# Foreign V

A collection of short stories

# Foreign Voices

A collection of short stories

By Philip Charter

*For my father*

# Contents

# Introduction

Welcome to Foreign Voices, my first collection of short fiction. These stories have previously been published in literary magazines and anthologies, but have been re-edited and collated here for your reading pleasure.

I'm not going to sell you the same tired old story — that I was a born storyteller, and have been writing ever since I was a child. However, I do believe that people process *life* as story. Scene and summary, dialogue, narration, description, voice and style, all apply to our past, present and futures. Taking the step into writing fiction has helped me process those stories and translate them for others. Hopefully, you will find some meaning in the stories I offer.

If you had asked me, years ago, what the purpose of short stories is, I would have shrugged my shoulders. You might be doing this now, while reading this introduction. The truth is, the short story is difficult. It is a challenge. Without the familiar length and structure that we learn from reading novels, readers can feel daunted by the task of processing narrative in just a few thousand words. With such busy and occupied lives, it's no wonder many people stick to reading what they know.

The form allows readers to explore genres and sample a great variety of themes and styles, but it can provoke more questions than it provides answers.

For me, the short story provides the opportunity to learn about the choices people make, the lives that they lead, and the way they interact with others in their world. I find myself thinking about them long after reading, whether they are tales of bleak Russian winters, or futuristic romances. *What did they mean? Why did they start and end where they did? What relevance do they have to my life?* In fiction, there is nothing like that moment of reflection you take after finishing a great story.

A common theme in this book is the importance of location. You'll find stories in this book set in the USA, Argentina, France, Mexico, Spain, North Africa, Russia and all over the UK. Not all of these stories include foreigners, but the characters often don't fit neatly into their surroundings. This is something I'm sure we have all experienced.

I hope you enjoy reading this book, and consider seeking out other examples of short fiction from the many great anthologies and collections available.

Philip Charter

# La Recoleta Cemetery

*First published in Page & Spine*

The two elderly ladies met in the cemetery on the first day of the month. They walked the narrow pathways between the crypts of the statesmen, writers and humanists of the great city of Buenos Aires. Before they shared their news and caught up on the local happenings, they paid their respects. They believed it the proper way to do things.

That day, the sky was heavy, and Delfina Martinez commented as much to her friend. Perhaps the weather would brighten later, she thought. Delfina was visiting the grave of Agustín, as she had done every month for the last twelve years. She stood vigil in her polished riding boots and silk headscarf. Her monthly visits brought her little enjoyment, and she rarely said anything to her late husband. What more was there to say after 38 years of marriage? Washing the marble facade and laying freshly cut lilies was beginning to feel less like a ritual and more like a chore.

Rosa Paolini was pleased about the weather. At least there wouldn't be as many tourists. The ladies would have the place to themselves for a while. Rosa came to La Recoleta for a different purpose: to visit the grave of her idol, Eva Perón. The silly film that brought so many tourists to the cemetery didn't capture the real Evita. As a girl, Rosa had met Peron, and through her kind words and her honest smile, knew exactly who Eva María Duarte de Perón was, and what she stood for. It gave Rosa the strength to carry on after she had suffered her own family tragedy — a child who left and never came back. Perón's ideals were something worth fighting for, even sixty years later when Argentina insisted on walking the wrong path. Rosa looked very different from her heroine. She had square shoulders and fleshy features, and wore a floral dress that looked like a shop curtain. A few silver hairs glinted through her single black plait.

The Peróns wanted to empower people like her — working class Argentines from the poorer *barrios*. It gave Rosa a thrill to visit La Recoleta, and see the shining light sitting amongst the old-money dinosaurs. Even though Rosa's husband was still alive, the Paolini family could never afford such a lavish resting place for their lost son. Plots in the old city cemetery were strictly limited. The nineteenth century walls were already bulging with rich *porteños*, each trying to outdo their neighbours with marble obelisks, ornate crosses and ever-higher domes.

After the two women had completed their visits, they met at the entrance by the towering white pillars, under the words *Expectamus Dominium*.

The sound of someone sobbing ghosted over from the chapel next to the cemetery gate. Delfina was horrified to see a boy of about seven in such despair. She watched as the boy smudged tears across his face with his sleeve. He was an immigrant, Peruvian or

Bolivian probably. She tapped her friend and nodded towards the boy.

'*Mira. Pobrecito.*'

Rosa thought he might be lost, but the boy's father emerged from the chapel with leaden feet. He held an incense stick in one hand, and gripped the hand of his daughter with the other. The little girl, too young to understand, looked from brother to father, and father to brother. The family huddled together, saying nothing, looking in no particular direction, all waiting for someone to direct their next move. No one else left the chapel. They were the only ones at the funeral.

Rosa felt tears forming in her eyes and gripped Delfina's shoulder. Life in Argentina could be so cruel. The ladies looked on in silence. Delfina struggled to bury the apple-sized lump in her throat. There was something about the charged sky, and the cool air of the early morning that felt poignant, like God himself was trying to say something.

Without saying a word, the young father laid the incense stick down and shuffled off. He and the girl walked along the long path that led to the street. He looked back at his son to indicate that he should follow. The boy, still snivelling, ran towards his family, leaving the ladies to themselves once again.

The women stood and took in the morning air. It felt cleansing. Both of them would have liked a fresh start. After every visit, Delfina felt like she was escaping prison, and Rosa left even more convinced that Buenos Aires was heading for disaster.

Delfina took her companion by the arm, and they walked up and down the undulations of the Plaza de Francia. The crouching trees and cut pathways encircled the walls of La Recoleta; providing a calming sea of green between the cemetery and the high-rise blocks around. Burning charcoal filled the air with the smell of wood smoke, as a vender wafted the the grill of his *choripan* stand. He was the only other soul in the park. After a few more minutes, the sun began to pierce the thick cloud and enhance the reds and yellows of the flowers.

Rosa suggested they stop for a coffee in Bar Manuelito, and the ladies set off towards their habitual resting spot. In a way, the café was similar to La Recoleta; it had a kind of crumbling beauty, and brought people from different walks of life together. If it wasn't cared for, it would be replaced by something brash and ugly, just like everything else in the city.

Though they had been friends for years, the women couldn't have been more different. Delfina, a retired psychologist, spent lonely days reading in her apartment in Palermo Hollywood. Her husband was gone, her son had moved to Spain, and even her pet Cocker Spaniel was dead. Some days, the only other person she spoke to was the doorman. Rosa was from La Boca, the southern *barrio* known for once declaring independence from the state. She could usually be found out in her small courtyard, trying to stop her neighbours' children from kicking the football into her washing.

The ladies took their places in the front window of Manuelito's café; that way they could keep an eye on the park. Rosa noted that the only thing that had changed about the cafe in the last twenty years was the price. Forty pesos for coffee and croissants was quite an extravagance.

Both women had suffered loss: Delfina with her husband, and Rosa, whose only boy had disappeared during the dictatorship. After years of investigation, she never got to the bottom of what had happened to him. Her meagre income was all that kept the family afloat, but once a month, she took time to come to La Recoleta, to visit Evita, and pray for her son, wherever he may lie.

While they sipped their coffees, they contemplated the situation with the grieving family. Delfina and Rosa had different views on immigration, however, they both agreed that life dealt a worse hand to some than to others. All you could do was thank God for whatever you still had: your family, your independence, your health.

Although the two friends only met once a month, they awoke each morning and sent a smiley face on their phones to check the other was well. They talked for an hour and avoided tricky topics such as politics or death, sticking to the changeable weather, upcoming events and even football (of course they supported rival teams).

Rosa insisted on paying the bill which embarrassed Delfina. She was a proud woman who deserved more recognition for living an honest life among such tragedy and poverty. Delfina thanked her friend, and changed the topic. There was to be another attempt at developing La Boca port.

Rosa was sceptical. '*Tsst. El dinero siempre desaparece.*' As she went into more detail about the port project, and how the money would soon be reassigned, Delfina's thoughts drifted back to what she'd seen at the chapel. She was stuck on that Bolivian family — the broken little boy and the father in denial. Delfina remembered the feeling well. She'd had no one to comfort her; only the pots of food provided by her neighbours, who gave pitying stares. She hadn't eaten a single one.

'. . . *y viajes a Patagonia, a Uruguay . . .*' Rosa continued.

Delfina hadn't taken a boat trip in a long time, but experiencing the cool breeze and the open water of the Rio del Plata suddenly seemed important. The trip would give her something to look forward to. She pictured the little girl's face when she had emerged holding her father's hand; too innocent to understand anything but the present. Wasn't that the best way? Agustín was gone, and her son hadn't been back for years. It was time to move forward. She would book a trip for the first day of next month.

'*Cuando fueron tus ultimas vaccaciones, Rosa?*' asked Delfina.

Rosa looked up, surprised that Delfina had joined the conversation. Holidays were not for the likes of the Paolinis. Her husband wasn't mobile, and they hadn't travelled anywhere since their honeymoon.

Delfina smiled and said it was time for Rosa to take a break. '*Ya es tiempo, Rosa.*'

The money wasn't important, and Delfina didn't mind where they went, as long as it was by boat. They could even head all the way up to Rio de Janeiro on a cruise. It would be carnival soon. She spent the next twenty minutes convincing her friend to accompany her.

Rosa was torn; she enjoyed listening to Delfina sing her praises, but she was anchored to La Boca. She felt guilty enough leaving Walter once a month, to come to the cemetery. Who knew how much longer he would be around? She understood how precious family moments could be, before your future together was torn away. Yet Rosa felt that somehow, she owed it to that poor family to be positive and look forward. She promised to think it over.

By the time they arrived back at their respective apartments — Delfina in Palermo Hollywood, and Rosa at her apartment in La Boca — the ladies were exhausted. Each meeting in the cemetery seemed like the opening and closing of a very old book, yet today, finally, they were reading the same story. It was the story of a cemetery and of a great city that had always flowed and changed with time, but was constantly under threat. Delfina was ready to face those threats. She wanted more than ever to value the present and to move on, not fearing what would happen next.

The next morning, when Delfina checked her phone, she saw that there was a message from Rosa and, next to the smiley face, was a picture of a little sailing boat.

# Godfrey Loses his Voice

*Highly Commended in the Sapiens Plurum
Earth Day 2018 Competition*

*First published in The Corona
Book of Science Fiction*

Speaking wasn't fashionable any more. Fifteen words a day was the most anyone would tolerate. It used to be fifteen thousand. Verbal communication had dwindled during the organic technology boom in the mid twenty-first century, and after that, device-aided *thought-to-text* took over. The art of conversation wasn't dying, it was dead.

Godfrey bounded up the old stone steps into the British Museum. He waved to the stoic security guard and decided today was the day to break the invisible sound barrier between them. 'Afternoon,' he offered. The security guard glared back at him as if one of the exhibits had just come to life. It was not the reaction Godfrey had hoped for.

Talking was ugly, naked, shameful. Many people never uttered a single word. Why bother? Implanted 'communicators' did everything for you. The extra-visual displays were convenient; they gave you time to formulate responses with reason checkers built in. Most people only talked to request a P.C.I. (Personal Communication Identifier), and used a set phrase. 'Good day, Citizen. Please provide P.C.I.'

For Godfrey, the biggest shame wasn't that no-one spoke anymore, it was that nobody listened. None of his classmates listened. They made fun of his insistence on *speech-to-text* because he didn't want his command history logged.

Obikwelu, Godfrey: [*disable communicator*]

GovNet S35 communicator: [*DISABLE . . . ARE YOU CERTAIN?*]

Godfrey: [*Y*]

GovNet S35 communicator: [*INCOMING REQUESTS TO BE DISABLED. LOGIC GATES OFFLINE. CONFIRM COMMAND . . .*]

Godfrey: [*Confirm*]

GovNet S35 communicator: [*DEVICE WILL REMAIN ONLINE FOR 60 SECONDS BEFORE SHUTDOWN*]

The museum was one of the only places where history wasn't updated every ten nanoseconds. Godfrey could read about ancient civilisations and feel a sense of space and time. He looked around the main vestibule, with its marble floors and serene classical music. The dome-ceilinged library, which had been restored some years ago, was his afternoon sanctuary. Why couldn't his school be like this, instead of dark cubicles and distance learning?

Glenda, the old custodian, smiled and beckoned him over to the central desk with a white glove. She was the head of Godfrey's recreational speaking group. He looked forward to the meetings, especially because Stefan would be there.

'Howdy Glenda. How's the library been?'

Several readers sitting at the neat rows of desks raised their eyes at the sound of an unabashed voice.

Glenda pointed and they walked in silence over to the modern-classics literature section.

'Ah, can't complain,' she said in her soft Scottish tone. 'What'll we read today, eh?'

'I'll carry on with Harry Potter,' he said, straightening up a little, like a dog hoping for a pat on the head. 'Hope I can finish it today.'

One of the regular scholars looked like he was going to say something, but he refrained.

'I'll go and get it for you, pet. You stick to the original version. None of this optimised stuff.'

Godfrey nodded.

Glenda brought the book, and Godfrey settled down at one of the old wooden desks to read.

Ninety minutes passed, with Godfrey repositioning himself in his seat after each chapter, fiddling with his thick framed glasses — yet another anachronism. The school forums were full of posts about the '20th century kid', and his 'goggles.' He didn't care. He had told his mum to use her Credits to upgrade his brother Ngozi's ocular implant. He could do without.

A touch on his shoulder startled him, and brought him back to the present day. Back to the buildings fighting for space and the choking dusty air.

'It's five-thirty, pet,' whispered Glenda. 'You looked away with the fairies.'

'Wizards more like,' he said. 'Only twenty pages to go now.'

'Aye, well it'll still be here tomorrow.'

Godfrey looked at the light pouring through the glass-domed ceiling and wondered if you could still even study to be a custodian. He handed the book over and waved goodbye. 'See you tomorrow.' He wished he could stay, and watch the workings of the library, each book carefully stored in beautiful order.

Godfrey walked past the security guard into the thick evening air. Best turn it back on.

Godfrey [*Communicator: Start*]
The usual menus and options appeared instantly in Godfrey's display.
GovNet S35 communicator: [*ONLINE. UPDATE V59.7 SUCCESSFUL*]

Another update? They were so frequent now.

GovNet S35 communicator: [NEW *I.M. WAITING . . .*]
Mother: [*MegaMarket list: meat substitute 800g, pasta 1kg, two tins ready tomatoes, four breakfast packs, three litres milk*]

How was he supposed to carry all of that home? Godfrey wasn't even sure he had enough Credits for the entire list. It would be at least eighteen thousand. MegaMarket still charged for drone delivery, so his mum made him shop in person, fighting through the V.R. ads and offers.

Godfrey would have to walk around Regent's Park, which was really just a building site, the construction bots to-ing and fro-ing, belching cement particles into the air. There was no way London was adhering to air quality standards.

Godfrey passed the New Euston Heights development with its lush vertical gardens. Impressive, how the other half lived. No

Monday commuters yet, just a few mothers and couples scurrying along with their heads down, plugged into their conversations.

After a couple more turns, Godfrey stopped and took a seat on a low brick wall. He slowed his breathing, looking forward to the filtered MegaMarket air. It seemed funny that there used to be so much open space, that the world used to be flat and not vertical.

He channeled his communicator. 'New note,' he said clearly.

GovNet S35 communicator: [*COMMAND NOT RECOGNISED*]

'New note,' he said again, imitating his best Queen's English.

GovNet S35 communicator: [*COMMAND NOT RECOGNISED. VOICE COMMAND NOT SUPPORTED*]

What? Apart from his weekly conversation club, his communicator was the only 'person' he spoke to. Why had they removed it? He hadn't agreed to new terms of use. GovNet couldn't just take away your power of speech could they? It wasn't legal. 'Show update changes,' he ordered.

GovNet S35 communicator: [*COMMAND NOT RECOGNISED*]

He tutted. Bloody hell. He entered the text.

Godfrey: *[Show update changes]*

The new settings appeared in his projection.
*[UPDATE V59.7: VOICE COMMAND INDEFINITELY SUSPENDED DUE TO SECURITY BREACH. THOUGHT-TO-*

*TEXT AND MANUAL INPUTS AVAILABLE]*

Why hadn't he heard about this? Despite the fact that not many people used the speech function anymore, it was the only non-monitored input. Godfrey looked around for a bystander sympathetic to his cause, but he was alone in a residential street with only bolted flat blocks and grey pavements for company. He made a mental note to ask Stefan if he knew anything.

\*\*\*

Godfrey was early to the meeting. He paced up and down replaying the same questions in his mind. Why hadn't Stefan responded? They normally shared everything. No more groups above twenty people, location data tracking, and now forcing people to run all communication through GovNet servers. Surely there was some kind of legal failsafe to stop this happening.

'Security measures' covered everything they wanted to take away. They might be able to filter through your entire command history, but face-to-face conversations were still private.

The Speaking Time conversation club, met every Tuesday evening in St. Mary's Church, Islington. Godfrey took a seat, rested his hands on his knees and waited for the others to arrive.

Most of the group were over seventy, some over ninety. Godfrey didn't mind. He got on quite well with Henry (when he wasn't grumbling about lungs), and Pamela usually brought cakes. Glenda, the elderly Scottish librarian, chaired the meetings.

Stefan arrived at exactly 2000 hours and took a seat next to Godfrey. He was the only young person Godfrey knew that dared to talk. Due to his position in the Legacy Ministry, he had to maintain a healthy interest in the past. They made an odd team — Stefan, tall, Nordic, with a cropped white side parting, and

Godfrey, a skinny black kid with a corkscrew mop. They greeted each other with their customary special handshake.

'Well? Did it happen to you too?' Godfrey said, still clasping his friend's hand.

'Hello Godfrey,' he said with his perfect BBC accent. 'What's happened?'

'The update,' said Godfrey, looking around, as if the new software was listening in. 'Didn't you get my I.M. about speech-to-text?'

'Yeah, sorry. I . . . I suppose it's not that weird. You are the only person I know who actually uses it.'

'But why shut it down?'

'We don't get told everything, but some things are for our own security.' Stefan tapped his nose. 'Remember the attacks last y—'

'That was the only command data GovNet didn't have access to. Speech.'

'Well. What are you worried about? You think they want to know what's on your shopping list?'

'MegaMarket already has a good handle on that.' Godfrey frowned and drummed his fingers on his knee.

Some other group members arrived and sat down. Stefan watched them with interest.

'Who have you been talking to, about the update?'

'Just my chat groups. They don't think anything of it, but I'll find people who care. It can't be legal.'

Stefan drew breath. He put on his 'big-brotherly' voice. 'Be careful, buddy, don't go raising a fuss.'

Godfrey couldn't believe it. He was sure that someone as smart as Stefan would understand. 'It's just a play by Gov—'

Glenda stood up to begin the meeting. 'Welcome, everyone. Today we will start with our lecture by young Godfrey, then move on to some pronunciation exercises with the audio, then finally onto free speech.'

The older members of the group seemed satisfied that all was correct with the schedule. They smiled at Godfrey, who sat in his checked shirt, with his clunky spectacles. He fitted right in.

'Do I have to stand up?' he asked.

'No, pet,' replied Glenda. 'You do as you want.'

He straightened his chair, and brought up the notes on his communicator. As he opened his mouth, ready to deliver his rehearsed opening to The World's Greatest Museums, he stopped. Godfrey looked at the grey-haired, kind-eyed pensioners looking back. 'Well, I . . . I was going to talk about my prepared subject — museums, but something is happening. Something major.'

The elderly faces showed no sign of alarm. Stefan shifted in his seat, observing the group's reaction.

Godfrey continued. 'Has anyone tried the *speech-to-text* function since last night?'

No one replied.

'It's gone.' He looked down. 'Not there anymore.' There was a silence in the church.

'Just the usual system updates,' said Stefan, raising a hand. 'Nothing to worry about.'

Godfrey glared at him, then continued. 'Don't you know what this means?'

Henry sprang into action. 'It's got problems.' He cleared his throat. 'It can't understand many people now. Such disparate accents, such nasty pronunciation. They must be improving it.'

'No,' said Godfrey firmly. 'That's not it. It's been removed for our 'security'.'

Stefan joined in with Henry. 'It's buggy, has been for years. Voice patterns are too hard to detect now.'

Henry nodded, vindicated.

Godfrey stood up, trying to rouse the troops. 'Do you know what was different about *speech-to-text*?'

Pamela shrugged.

'It was the final private data entry method for communicators. GovNet didn't have access to the input data.'

Pamela shrugged again. 'But we all use the other inputs, love.'

Stefan looked distant, like his brain was in another room, he was making notes on his communicator. 'As someone who works at the ministry, I can reassure you all that security updates are necessary to protect us from the threat of attack.'

'That sounds reasonable,' said Glenda, trying to calm Godfrey down with a sympathetic look.

Godfrey sighed. 'This group is the final private communication left.'

She nodded, closing her eyes. 'Aye, I know, laddie. That's why we need to keep it going.'

'Exactly,' said Godfrey. 'And, get more members. Put the word out.'

'No one wants to join us old fogies,' grumbled Henry. 'We're fighting a losing battle. People run a mile rather than speak to me nowadays.' He doubled over in one of his coughing fits after finishing the sentence.

'Can we put it on the agenda for next week? Increasing membership?' asked Godfrey.

The group grumbled in agreement, and the meeting continued as normal.

*** 

None of Godfrey's classmates thought *speech-to-text* was a pressing issue. He had brought this up during his scheduled meetings with the counsellor but non-engagement wasn't bullying.

If people didn't want to communicate with Godfrey, that was their choice. No teenager in their right mind wanted to interact with a freak who liked practicing a dead art of speaking. Who wanted to hang out in a church full of senior citizens? Nobody. Speaking Time seemed destined to remain at only seven members, with a couple of them too ill to come.

At least Stefan was there for Godfrey. They chatted every day via I.M., and Stefan had offered to help spread the word about Speaking Time (although he hadn't attended the last meeting). It was only a matter of time before more members walked through the church doors.

It was a Sunday, and they had arranged at a café in Midtown. This one had a physical server and non-automated ordering. One of the walls was covered with hessian coffee sacks, and the others streamed live videos of endless Colombian hillsides. It was amazing how the formatting tricked your brain. What with the *finca*-fresh aroma, the piped birdsong, and the light breeze, you could actually be there.

He ordered a chocolate milk and Stefan got a coffee with nutrition boost. Godfrey's eyes bulged at the price — 12,000 Credits. The server keyed in the orders and the drinks were transported to their table before they could even sit down.

'How have you been?' asked Godfrey.

His voice cut through the quiet like a buzz saw.

The only other customers in the café, a middle-aged couple, nearly spat out their coffee. They shot laser beam looks at Godfrey and Stefan.

'Let's use I.M. We'll only disturb people here,' said Stefan, lowering the volume.

'But, we said. Vocalising is best.'

'It just attracts too much attention, buddy.'

17

Godfrey sighed and switched his communicator on. He connected with Stefan.

Godfrey: [*When can we post? We can make a difference. You know how fast things spread through connection groups*]
Stefan: [*You can't seed ideas directly. I know you are not a real threat, but you've got to stop*]

Godfrey took a long pull on the straw of his chocolate milk. Why had he bothered to walk all the way into town? He could be getting this lecture at home instead of in a Colombian café.

Godfrey: [*Why don't you come to the group anymore? We are planning on going out on the streets to sign up members. We need everyone there*]
Stefan: [*I can't come, it's not possible with work now. We're location monitored and the group has been logged*]
Godfrey: [*Logged?*]

Stefan looked up and sighed. He put both hands flat on the steel table.

Stefan: [*I didn't want to be the one to tell you this. It's over. The group is finished. I was ordered by my superior to attend the meetings . . . to watch you*]

Godfrey felt a pain in his chest. He couldn't breathe. His best friend, the only person he had trusted, had been spying all along. He looked away from the traitor and focussed instead on the expansive greens and browns of the coffee plantations that swayed in perfect three dimensions. He suddenly felt very small.

Godfrey: [*This is fun for you, isn't it? Reporting back to the government about a funny little geek. All I've got is the group*] Stefan: [*I like you, kid, but I'm sorry to say you are on your own. Nobody uses voice. Nobody will. Not any more*]

Godfrey's links to the pre-tech world were severed, officially. He pushed his expensive chocolate milk into the middle of the table.

Godfrey: [*I've got nothing to lose. I'll keep trying—*] 'Why am I texting this? I can speak when I want.'

The couple looked up again. The woman shushed him.

'Shush yourself. Too chicken to talk? Your life is filtered, monitored, optimised . . . fake!'

'Godfrey, stop.' Stefan raised a finger.

'I will fight this Stefan. I'll make a new group.'

Stefan stopped talking. He nodded, signalling another I.M. communication.

The couple withdrew their outraged expressions.

Stefan [*Will you attempt to organise counter-culture groups over twenty people?*]

'Yes. Screw you, Stefan. I will speak with the others, and I will organise a group. GovNet can't get away wi—'

Those were the last words that Godfrey ever said. A sound cut him off. It was a short sonic pulse. Stefan sat in total calm, with a small silver device, about the size of a pen, directed at Godfrey's throat.

What was that thing? Godfrey brought a hand up to his neck. A new message appeared.

GovNetS35 communicator: [*ORAL STERILISATION OF OBIKWELU GODFREY, PCI 35D243525JKI COMPLETED.*

19

*MESSAGE DELETED*]

Godfrey looked at Stefan, his eyes burning with questions, pleading him to do something. He tried to protest, but nothing came out. Not even a whimper.

Stefan stood up and put the device back into his pocket. As he laid a hand on Godfrey's shoulder he said aloud, 'I'm sorry.' He left without another word. He never even glanced back.

\*\*\*

Godfrey never spoke again, but he wrote. He wrote this story and copied the text onto paper every morning. Each day, he left it in a different location — sometimes in a café, sometimes in an office block, and sometimes he gave it to the first person he heard speak that day. Now that you have read it, he asks that you do the same.

# Freewheeling

*First published in Sentinel Literary Quarterly*

Luke was looking forward to the punishment. The only time he felt in control was when his leg muscles were burning and his lungs were screaming for air. He had the right amount of grit and determination to be a half-decent cyclist, although he didn't get out as much as he would like. But after daydreaming about racking up the kilometres all week, he was free now, if only for a few hours.

He filled his water bottles in preparation for the North African heat.

'How's work looking for next week?' asked Gabby.

'It's going slowly, love. We've hit a roadblock with another community that wants to be 'compensated for the disruption of the new pipelines.''

'God. People have always got their hand out here.'

'Well it's not that sim—'

'I thought it would be wrapped up by now and we would be on our way home.' She always cut him off, and now she was pregnant, she was even less patient. Luke wasn't against having kids, it just wasn't the right time. The last conversation they'd had about children ended without a firm resolution, but a few weeks later she had announced the pregnancy.

'How long have you been tinkering? I swear you pay more attention to that thing than you do to me.'

Luke looked up from his brake callipers, like he'd been caught in bed with another woman. 'Just getting ready to go out. I'm doing the whole loop today.'

Gabby pursed her lips. 'What time will you be back? Greg and Amanda are coming for dinner.'

'I didn't forget, I'll be back to help I promise, just don't expect me to cycle down to the shops if you forget anything. Not after six hours in the saddle.'

She sighed a tired sigh, 'I don't know how much longer I can do this on my own Luke.'

He froze. 'Do what on your own?'

'This.' She waved an arm towards the heat outside the window. 'I'm pregnant if you haven't noticed, and I don't want to bring a child up in this, this dust bowl. I want to have the baby back home.'

'But we talked about this, Love, we agreed.' Luke touched Gabby's cheek. 'We've got everything we need here. It's no good for a family to be apart.'

'I just want what's best for the baby.' She was raising her voice now.

'And I want what's best for this family. Look, let's talk about this when I get back, okay?'

'Mmm, later . . .' She gave him a peck on the cheek, leaning from a distance because of the baby bump. She always kissed that side to avoid the pink scar to the right of his eye. Luke hoped it looked like a Viking battle wound, but most people thought he had some kind of growth on his face. Gabby encouraged him to wear his sunglasses for photos. The Bond villain scar had come from a fight that he had lost with a burglar in his own Yorkshire home. Really, it was the crowbar that won the fight. The kid had scarpered in fear and was never caught. There was no damage to his eye, but people always stared.

Over the past few months, he had been working up to this ride, ratcheting up the distance. The route in question was a one hundred and forty kilometre loop with a lot of cumulative elevation. It had been used as a stage on the World Tour a few years back. He wasn't physically gifted, but Luke was determined, and that goes a long way in cycling. He carried his bike down the stairs and asked the doorman to open the compound gate. Freedom.

The wheels cut a path down the road, the air rushing past his ears. The rear cassette spun like a football clacker as he freewheeled around the bends. The roads weren't as bad as they used to be, although the tarmac laid down before the big race was starting to crack. He looked out for potholes and stray rocks.

On the way back up, Luke maintained a steady pressure, driving the gears, up to eighty revolutions a minute in his hill climbing gear. As he snaked up the incline, a pickup truck struggled alongside him. A gangly teenager sat in the back, staring.

'Come on round.' He motioned for it to overtake.

The vehicle nudged ahead, engine screaming, its thick exhaust fumes engulfing Luke. It eventually got in front and disappeared over the brow of the hill. Luke clenched his teeth and chased it.

At the top, the treeline broke and a vast, lunar mountain range appeared. The tiny buildings looked like they had been sprinkled from a great height. Some tiny white specks shifted in a dusty field. Luke looked up at the high sun and started down the slope.

As Luke's speed increased, so did his confidence. Up to almost seventy kilometres per hour, he didn't want to lose momentum. He gripped the brake levers and ducked down to minimise air resistance. According to his cycle computer, he was about two thirds of the way round the course and making good time.

The road was starting to flatten out, and Luke snaked left past a small group of mud brick houses. The bend was tighter than it first appeared and the bike drifted out, toying with a shallow ditch. Luke fought to keep the bike on tarmac, but the front wheel entered the jaws of the trap at too high a speed. It dug into the dirt and Luke felt the rim crack under the pressure of the impact. He had no chance of controlling the fall. As he tried to unclip his shoes from the pedals, a thought flashed into consciousness. Instead of thinking of his wife, his family or his unborn child, the blurry face of his teenage assailant with the crowbar came into focus. He flew through the air, finally separated from his charge; straining to protect his face rather than relaxing for impact in order to avoid broken bones. He shut his eyes.

A splash of cool water brought him back around. His neck and arm and chest hurt. Must be the collarbone. Luke got to his feet and checked his appendages with a shaking hand, they all seemed all there. His cycling top was torn at the arm and sticking to his chest. He was wet through — a large puddle had cushioned his fall and reduced the damage. He hobbled towards the buildings on the corner, his plastic cycling shoes clip-clopping on the tarmac.

\*\*\*

The old man raised the teapot high, pouring the steaming liquid with pinpoint accuracy. By now, the process was ritual, each step performed with perfect form. Luke picked up the glass with his good hand, and blew on the tea. His other arm was cradled in a sling, held in place by two large safety pins.

'*A salaam alaikum*,' said Luke. 'You're very kind.' He leaned back in the armchair.

The old man grinned back at him with crooked teeth. There were four more glasses to fill. He squatted down with the legs of a much younger man. Yazir and Fatima, the couple, sat together on the sofa in plain robes, hands on knees. Their child played with his big tuft of black hair. He couldn't have been more than five, but he already had his own little cup, the tea cooling next to the others. He stared at the foreigner in silence, his gaze fixed on Luke's scar.

'D'où êtes-vous, l'Espagne?' asked Yazir.

'England. *Angleterre*. Sorry. *Je ne pas Francais*.'

'Ahh Englan' . . . very good. *Musique*.'

'Yes, yes. Do you have a telephone?' said Luke making a mobile shape with his hand.

'Le Queen. Le Champions. Good.' Yazir was still thinking of other British rock songs he knew.

Past the mud brick doorway lay two bedrooms and a kitchen just big enough to hold the range and some pots. A breeze blew through the open window and Luke could hear goats clattering around in the pen outside.

After a few back and forth gestures, it turned out that they didn't have a phone, but there was a neighbour who might be able to help. Luke was old enough that he remembered the time before phones, without the distractions and interference.

Gabby begged him to take his mobile when he went out. He could just imagine her saying, 'What if you get lost, or need help? What then?' She even put it in his back pocket once, but he took it out before leaving. He was going to get the full 'I told you so' now. Even with the cycle computer, the carbon fibre bike, the electrolyte drink and breathable fabric, Luke was now at the mercy of a goat herder's neighbour, who was seemingly out. This might be the end of the unaccompanied rides into the wilderness.

He settled back into the chair and tried to rest. There wouldn't be much traffic passing on a Sunday evening. He would have to wait and see. Yazir got up to look at the broken wheel, tea in hand. He tutted and shook his head.

The sun was setting, bathing the hills in purples and yellows, but before it went down, the family insisted on giving Luke the full tour. It was a spectacular location, nestled between mountain ridges. As well as introducing Luke to the goats, Yazir showed off his pride and joy: the vegetable garden. Luke had had to fight for space in his own pokey kitchen in order to install a few pots of herbs. Now he stood before this veritable oasis.

The garden was planned to perfection, every available space used. A pump handle well fed irrigation channels running between the plants. Luke wanted to test the pumping mechanism, but his neck and shoulder still hurt from the fall. The sunflowers, beans, and squashes peered out from between thick leaves.

Inside Luke showed his cycle computer to Yazir and his little son. 'It's only forty-two kilometres back to the city,' he said.

The boy was more interested in trying to get into one of the energy gel sachets. Yazir snatched the packet from his mouth.

After dinner, the neighbour arrived. Thankfully he spoke a smattering of English. He held his woolen waistcoat trying to catch his breath under his thick beard.

'Hello, my friend, I Hamid. What your name?'

'I'm Luke. It's nice to meet you.' He smiled sheepishly, pointing to his collarbone, not able to offer his hand.

'Where you come by, the city?'

'Yes I need to get back to my wife in the city.' He made the rounded sign of a pregnant belly.

Hamid looked at the family, raising an eyebrow.

'You have telephon' number your wife?'

Luke scrolled through his memory, but his wife's number wasn't in the rolodex. 'Err, you can call the office.' He asked for a pen and paper and wrote the following note:

*Luke Robson had a cycling accident and is unable to come into work. He will return to the office when transport is available.'*

'Can you read it OK?'

'Yes yes, my friend, I call wife okay?'

'No no, it's my office, the *office*. My company. You understand?'

Hamid looked blank.

Luke wrote down the team secretary's name and number and prayed the message would get through.

*\*\*\**

The smell of fresh bread filled the lounge. Luke's shoulder still hurt but he felt rested after a night on the sofa. The old man was scurrying back and forth with the tea set, whilst Fatima toasted some type of pancakes on a griddle.

Hamid burst in through the wooden door, ducking as he entered.

'My friend, your wife call many time.' His eyes were lit up. 'She say no working today.'

'Tell her I will get home when I can.' Luke looked out of the door at the road. It wasn't worth going all the way to the neighbour's farm to speak with her on the fixed line. The trucks would start passing soon.

The old man offered tea to Hamid. He drank it standing up, hopping from foot to foot, babbling about important neighbourhood business.

Yazir and the boy were dressed and ready for the day ahead.

27

'Good morning,' Luke greeted them as they came in. 'Thank you again for your hospitality,' he clasped his hands together. He wanted to give the family something to thank them, but had nothing with him. A grander gesture was needed. 'Can I help with your goats today?' he suddenly found himself offering. They would welcome an extra pair of hands, and it would be easy enough to get back to the city later. What was the rush? He didn't feel able to struggle through meetings, with all of their handshakes and smiles. Apart from the grazes and sore collarbone, Luke was enjoying his freedom. Herding goats would be more fun than his usual Monday business.

Hamid translated the offer of help to Yazir. The old man looked at his son and they laughed. Yazir slapped Luke on the back and pointed out toward the field.

After breakfast, the men headed out to drive the goats towards greenery. It was no easy task, the hills were barren and the air was still. At least it was early, before the heat of the day.

'*Yalla, yalla.*' Yazir directed the goats, giving the stragglers an occasional tap with his stick. Luke held the right flank, Yazir was on the left and the boy in the middle, all marching along. The boy watched Luke's awkward shuffling steps in his borrowed sandals.

After nearly an hour of stopping and starting, they reached a small hill covered with scrubby plants and patches of brown grass. Breakfast had arrived for the goats, who consumed whatever they could. They stripped the leaves from low lying bushes and plants like they were pulling the meat off a kebab skewer. This was all so simple — no protracted negotiations, no forms to sign in triplicate, and no need to think about the digital requirements and social media implications. The goats just ate.

'What's that?' Luke pointed out a small wooden sign.

Yazir smiled. 'For sale. Hamid sale.'

It hadn't even crossed his mind that people bought and sold land here. The quiet life must be pretty cheap, maybe a few thousand for a decent plot. Luke suddenly imagined himself marshalling his own herd, calling the names one by one. The more time he spent here, the more he dreaded the return to to the air conditioned compound.

An idea started to take shape in Luke's mind. He had always wanted his own project. He wanted to provide the best life for his little family, and this was beautiful. Simple. It was as if the bright sunshine had scorched an imprint of the three of them there. Gabby would take some convincing, but Luke never backed down from a challenge.

The rocks were too hot to sit on, so they watched in silence. The animals swayed from side to side to keep them from overheating.

Luke rummaged around in his top pocket and extracted an energy packet. He pressed it into the hand of the boy, who looked at him wide-eyed. He ruffled the boy's hair. A photo would have been nice, but as he reached into his pocket to get his phone, Luke remembered it wasn't there.

When the herders returned, the family said their goodbyes and Yazir stayed with Luke to help flag down a passing car or truck. Luke stood in his bright cycling gear, much taller than the shepherd whose cotton robe reached his sandals. There was no sign of the crash from yesterday, no skid-marks, and no water on the road. It had evaporated. Luke's bike lay next to him waiting patiently. After half an hour, a brown lorry approached the bend and Yazir waved his arms, causing it to slow.

\*\*\*

Luke straightened his back and rested on his pickaxe handle.

Summer was coming to an end and he wanted to get planting in the hope he would have something to pull up by the end of the year.

Even after softening the ground, digging was tough. He had put the well in a week ago, using a contact at work to get an easy-to-install kit. The tranquil farm life that he had craved felt a lot like hard work now, with just a breeze and the occasional passing bird for company.

Gabby had sent a few messages, but they still hadn't spoken much. She used to be his biggest supporter, cheering him on during his cycling races back in England. Not anymore. She had someone more important to think about, someone he hadn't even met yet. Her baby wouldn't grow up in some underdeveloped backwater. Too hot. Too dry. *He* was being selfish.

Luke had tried. 'It needs a bit of work, but it's a wonderful place, great for a family,' he had said. 'Not too far from the city. You have to see it at least.'

'You're mad if you think I'm going out all that way to look at a piece of dirt. What will happen to the house back home? What about your parents, and mine? You're just not thinking straight.'

'That's it. I *am* thinking straight for once. We came here to make a new life. We don't need all the mod cons to be happy. The garden, the mountains, and such nice people. It's pure, Gabby.'

'I can't talk to you when you're being this pig-headed. If you do this, then you can count me out.' She folded her arms on top of her swollen stomach.

'You can't make threats like that.' Luke's voice was cracking. 'I've already committed to it. It's no money, and I'll still be working. I'll cycle in every day.'

'There's not even any mobile service out there. I had to call up that bloody madman four times to get a message to you.'

'Well you never miss these things when you don't—'

'Arrgghh! It's not up for discussion. I don't want to talk about it anymore.'

'So you're just giving up and going. I'm doing this for *us*. You know I can't come back with you because of the contract.' He didn't feel like it was selfish to want a simpler life, even if it was two against one.

Gabby was true to her word and had gone back to Yorkshire. She had cut him out of their lives. No calls, no messages. It was up to him to finish his work and return to reality. Nevertheless, Luke had spent his evenings and weekends preparing the house and the garden, getting ready for the arrival of his family in the hope that Gabby would change her mind. He still had eight months left on his work contract and was already thinking about whether to keep on going on the project or just cave.

He got the occasional progress report from the grandparents. *Mother and baby doing fine. Hang in there, you'll be home soon.* But, Luke already felt at home on his 'patch of dirt' in the mountains. He'd seen photos, but Luke felt like Gabby had conjured his son out of nowhere and stolen him away before he could even lay eyes on him. At least he felt at peace on the farm. They would be impressed at how far it had come, he sent regular updates.

He rubbed his eyes and thought about finishing up for the day. Why didn't he just call it quits? His family and friends had already rallied around Gabby and the baby, and his back and shoulders hurt from digging. Just another few meters would do, then he could pop over and see the neighbours. It had been a while since he'd delivered a new bike for the little boy; a thank you for everything they had done.

The sun was beginning to cast its shadow over the hills. Luke needed to rest before the ride into work tomorrow. He lifted the pickaxe and headed back towards the house. As he did, a familiar figure made his way across the field in his robe and sandals. Hamid held his *kufi* in place as he skipped towards him.

'Luke, Luke! Incredible.'

'What is it?'

'Mrs. Luke call me.'

'What? Are you sure? When?' It had been months since they had spoken. 'What did she say,' his heart was pounding.

'She say you call her.'

'She wants to speak?' Luke felt a surge of energy. 'Oh Hamid, I could hug you.'

He gripped his neighbour in a tight embrace. Hamid smiled, revealing a missing tooth.

'*Monsieur Luke. En y va.*' He turned and headed towards the road that led to his property, signalling for Luke to follow.

# Black Flowers

*First published in The Second*
*Corona Book of Horror Stories*

Sidney cut the roses with the secateurs and tossed the stems onto the pile on the floor. You had to cut them back hard to keep them fresh. Hopefully, it would turn things around for the wilting flowers. Inside, the sparse drum beat of The Cure echoed through the florist's shop, as outside the streets bristled with Monday morning life.

Fulfilling orders, managing stock and arranging the displays: it was too much for one person. Worst of all, Sidney had to deal with the customers. One stood outside the front door now, peering in. An old bag in a headscarf rapped on the glass door.

'Are you open?' she asked, revealing an extraordinarily gummy mouth.

'No. Not yet.' Sidney hated early risers.

'Oh, well I'm ever so sorry to bother you but—'

The family had moved here from London for the peace and quiet, but it turned out that Truro was a town like any other — guilty men buying bouquets, rich city dwellers getting married nearby, and old people dying. There were lots of funerals in Cornwall. The toothless crone begging to be let in at 8.38am was probably here for funeral arrangements. The sign clearly stated the opening time of 9:30. 'What do ya' want?' asked Sidney, through the glass door.

It was Fran who had suggested opening a shop; flowers always sold, and people in this part of the world still valued the personal touch. Sidney had never been one for frilly things in life, but now Fran had moved back to London with Charlie, the only option was to hold things down until they saw sense and the family got back together.

The reluctant florist sighed and unlocked the front door. The bell jingled merrily as the woman scurried inside. Sidney made a mental note to take it off the door later. The woman wasted no time in sharing every detail of the 'worst week of her life'. Her Arthur was gone and there had been 'ever so much paperwork'. At least someone else was miserable too.

Why the hell should flower sellers have to smile and provide sparkling conversation? Especially when their family had abandoned them after one misunderstanding. It was only a few threats and a dead crow in the mail, for God's sake. Sidney had done it for *them*, to put a hex on the new shop sucking the life out of their family's business. But that was it — divorce pending and custody of Charlie gone. At least Fran had stopped short of citing the Mental Health Act. Sidney would show them things were getting better by making a success of the shop.

'It's a bit dreary in here, isn't it? And I don't like that music,' said the old lady, who turned out to be called Mrs Godbeer. 'Nasty smell too.'

Sidney looked down at her with contempt. 'It's eight-thirty. Haven't had a chance to bin the cuttings yet, and the music stays.'

'When I came in here last year the displays were colourful: lilies and carnations. And there was none of that voodoo stuff over there. It's unchristian.'

Bloody Bible bashers, thought Sidney. 'We're actually an alternative florists. Haven't you seen the new name? Black Flowers. We've got some nice dahlias, midnight pansies and black magic hollyhocks.'

Mrs Godbeer didn't look impressed.

'Listen, lady, times change. Black is the new black,' said Sidney, forcing a smile.

'Oh dear. I just need a basic wreath, you see.'

'I'd recommend one of our funeral packages. Take a pamphlet.'

'It's all a bit gothic for me. My Arthur loved bright colours, roses and the like. I think I better get a second opinion.'

What a waste of time, and after opening early for her as well. One way or another, the shop would convert this town of fussy traditionalists. Monochrome flowers could be beautiful too. 'Alright, Mrs Godbeer. You come back if you change your mind.' She was probably heading straight down to Occasions, to see that pandering ponce of a flower merchant, Prunella Smyth. She might think the war was over after the court upheld the restraining order, but Sidney was just getting started. Things had been much simpler when there was only the one florist in town.

Gummy Godbeer muttered something on the way out. Her friends in the Rotary Club wouldn't be passing by. Big deal. When gothic became fashionable again Black Flowers would make the magazines, and be heralded as a trailblazer.

It was somewhat strange that a practising Satanist had ended up as a florist. Cornwall's pagan tradition had always fascinated

Sidney, and things had been good for a while, then Fran voiced doubts about the books, the clothes and the spells. Apparently, some of the kids at school were teasing Charlie.

The people in Truro expected florists to look like Prunella Smyth – horsey women with perfect teeth and antique jewellery. They were unaccustomed to dealing with ungainly goths with spiky hair and skull rings like Sidney.

After work, Sidney went upstairs to the flat above the shop. Tomorrow was Tuesday, which was a busy day in Truro. With yet another delayed mortgage instalment due, Sidney considered making a few concessions to increase cash flow until the busier summer season started. Would it be best to remove the books, candles and amulets? No. It was important to push the agenda; not all florists should offer namby-pamby bouquets and conform to type.

To make matters worse, there was a leaflet from Smyth's shop smiling up from the doormat. Rage boiled. Was it not possible to fail in your personal and business life, and not have your face rubbed in it when you came home?

A well-worn copy of Poe's *The Murders in the Rue Morgue* lay open on the coffee table. Sidney knew every gory detail of the locked room murder. It had sparked an interest in death that had stayed with Sidney since reading it as a 16-year-old. A particular passage of text sprang to mind.

*...the party made its way into a small paved yard in the rear of the building, where lay the corpse of the old lady, with her throat so entirely cut that, upon an attempt to raise her, the head fell off.*

Tonight was not going to be another occasion for drowning sorrows with cheap beer and slasher movies. This situation was untenable. To produce new life you had to cut back the dead flesh.

What the business needed was a sacrifice, a real one this time, and it had to be tonight.

Sidney had killed animals before, slitting their throats and watching the life go out of their eyes, but somehow always knew it would come to this.

The kit was prepared, lying ready in the bathroom cabinet. Sidney recited a favourite Latin incantation, summoning the strength of Lucifer himself, then dressed in a long leather coat, grabbed the woollen hat lying on the hall table and headed out into the night.

What with the restraining order, it would be far too risky to approach the Smyth house without further planning, so it would be Mrs Godbeer who would play the role of the sacrificial flower tonight. In her sad and confused state, she'd probably thank Sidney for putting her out of her misery.

By the time Sidney entered the house, the whole town was silent. Truro wasn't exactly a late-night type of place. The lock on the back door was an old three lever – not difficult to jimmy open with the lock pick set. Sidney fitted the shoe covers, latex gloves and plastic cap. With no forensic evidence and no clear motive, even Poe's detective C. Auguste Dupin wouldn't have a chance in hell of solving the case.

Mrs Godbeer's galley kitchen smelled of sweet condensed milk. Sidney shuddered and moved into the carpeted lounge, careful not to displace any of the funeral cards sent by well-wishers. As expected, the old bat was upstairs, and snoring with metronome regularity.

The intruder towered over her, casting a shadow over the bed like a high priest at the altar on judgement day. *What a pathetic individual. She would have to do.*

'Dark Lord. Let this sacrifice bring renewal, vitality and success.'

Mrs Godbeer stirred, but continued her rhythmic breathing.

Without further hesitation, Sidney wrapped the ends of the florist's wire around specially padded gloves and plunged down upon the throat of the sleeping pensioner with a terrible force. The taut wire sliced deep into Mrs Godbeer's neck, crushing her windpipe and cutting into the flesh at each side of her neck. For the first time in a long time, Sidney felt in charge, powerful. Death was not something to be feared, but celebrated. Mrs Godbeer didn't even have time to open her eyes. It was over quickly. The old lady's feet jerked up one final time, and then she was still.

According to Poe's manuscript, the head must be completely severed, so Sidney set about cutting through the tissue with the razor-sharp knife from the sacrifice kit. In order to cut through the spine, Sidney used strong secateurs. Viscous blood leaked into the mattress of the double bed.

'*Et resurgent meae... Et resurgent mea*,' said Sidney, still a little out of breath.

It would be easy enough to dispose of the entire kit in the river on the way home. There were plenty of spares at the shop. The head was finally detached, and it rolled away from Mrs Godbeer's frail body.

As a final touch, Sidney left a single black rose in the glass on the bedside table. It looked perfectly macabre. Poe would have been proud. Of course, the police could trace it back to the shop, but that didn't mean anything. Mrs Godbeer had taken it as a sample after discussing arrangements for her husband's funeral. No evidence, no problem. Sidney left the house via the back door and stole into the night, satisfied with a ritual correctly performed.

* * *

After two months, Sidney had to admit that the sacrifice of Mrs Godbeer had not made a difference to the business. Fran still wasn't returning calls, and that bitch Smyth was still raking it in. Notices from Nairn's Debt Collectors were becoming ever more threatening.

In desperation, Sidney had even used the kit again, this time on an old boar of a man in Chacewater. He was a retired army colonel with a distastefully long moustache. He had said the shop 'legitimised Beelzebub' and should 'sell honest British flowers like chrysanthemums and poppies.' No one liked being told how to run their business. The colonel roared when the wire sliced through his leathery neck. Where was his God now? This time, Sidney had planted a neat row of midnight pansies in the front flower bed.

Of course, the police had made enquiries at the shop. A young female officer had taken notes. Yes, Mrs Godbeer had visited the shop and was a lovely old dear. She'd taken a sample of some flowers. Getting the arrangements right for her husband's funeral was a priority. It was important for the business too. Not everyone in Truro supported change. The shop had even had some sarcastic reviews online. The detective had sympathised, and had gone on her way.

The only way to break this run of bad luck was to eliminate the competition. It would have to be a clean job – there would be clear motive this time – but once Black Flowers was the only florist in town again, business would thrive. Fran and Charlie would come back after they saw how wonderful life in Truro could be. They could be a family.

That evening, Sidney prepared another kill kit. This third strike must surely be enough to satisfy the dark powers. All would be right after Prunella was gone. Sidney was doing the Dark Lord's work: cutting back the rotten flesh of society.

Approaching the door of Occasions, Sidney felt a charge of excitement, that familiar thrill of watching their souls leaving their sad bodies. Smyth would be in the flat above the shop, alone. Her husband was away on his weekly trip to Covent Garden Flower Market.

Occasions had a well-fitted front door and stout lock, so there was no point in trying to pick it this time. A small pane of glass cracked, then gave way with another hard elbow strike. Sidney entered and listened for any movement. Nothing. Pollen from the lilies on display choked the air. The padded carpet on the stairs would provide ample cushioning to disguise approaching footsteps.

Sidney nudged open the bedroom door and was surprised to find Prunella Smyth awake, lying in bed with her bedside light on. Even though she was supposed to be asleep by now, it didn't matter. The routine was well-practised – gloves on, cloth for padding and the thin wire. Now that posh trollop could say goodbye to her head.

'What the devil?' Prunella hoisted herself upright. She clutched something under the covers.

'It has to be you,' said Sidney, wrapping the wire around the gloves. 'The others didn't make a difference. He wants your blood.'

Prunella wore a panicked look on her face. She pulled the duvet up to her chest, as if being under the covers would somehow protect her. 'What are you doing here? This is my house, now, now get out. I shall call the—'

'I won't even have a house soon, you bitch. You and your poxy Occasions have ruined my business, my life.' Sidney was going to enjoy putting an end to this feud, and hoped that the Dark Lord would be pleased.

'Your Halloween shop makes a mockery of the business,' said Prunella. 'No wonder your customers come to me.'

'And look what happens to them.'

'What... Whatever do you mean?'

'Old Mrs Godbeer was rude about my displays, my black flowers—'

'You mean...? Oh dear God!' Prunella looked frantically for an escape route, but her path to the door was blocked.

'And that colonel in Chasewater too,' said Sidney.

Going into more details wasn't necessary. It was time to put an end to this. With arms outstretched, Sidney sprang forward. Prunella, eyes wide, squirmed to the side and managed to partially block the wire with her forearm. 'Wait!' The pressure opened a gash and blood oozed from the cut. Sidney grunted and lunged forward again. In a desperate attempt to avoid the wire making contact again, Prunella withdrew her right hand from under the covers, and raised a knitting needle in defence. As the wire drew closer, she plunged the sharp end into her assailant's neck. The needle went deep and Sidney was left pawing at the foreign object sticking out at a jaunty angle. Sidney staggered backwards, knocking over a vase in the process. Blood gushed from the wound in regular spurts. It must have hit an artery.

Prunella slumped back down onto the bed. It was self-defence. What were you supposed to do when your attacker lay floundering in their own blood on your bedroom floor? The police would believe her, they had to. The restraining order would provide all the backstory they would need. She got out of bed and darted to the opposite side of the room. There was no phone in the bedroom, so she ran to the office down the hall to inform the law. Prunella closed the door on her way out.

As Sidney stared up at the ceiling, holding the wound, blood seeped into the carpet and stained the fibres black. This wasn't how the story was supposed to end. Smyth had escaped with a minor wound, and it was the wrong florist who was clinging desperately to life.

Fran and Charlie would be sleeping soundly, unaware of the trouble their Sidney was going through to try and get their family life in Truro back on track. A dark veil began to draw over the room. They'd come back for the funeral, wouldn't they? Even with everything that had happened, they were family. The ceremony would be beautiful: an ebony coffin with white trim and wreaths from the shop – onyx tinted tulips, and rows and rows of beautiful black dahlias. With eyes now closed, Sidney prepared to make the journey to the underworld.

\*\*\*

*The Falmouth Packet,* 20th January
BRUTAL MURDER CASES SOLVED

Last night, Truro resident Prunella Smyth was attacked and injured in a home invasion, while her assailant Sidney Garbrandt was killed in self-defence. After breaking into Occasions, a florist's on Truro High Street, and attempting to strangle Mrs Smyth, Garbrandt, a woman with a history of mental health problems and a criminal record, died from the injuries she sustained in the struggle.

Garbrandt had previously threatened the owner of Occasions, who had obtained a restraining order against her. The dispute is thought to stem from the failure of Garbrandt's own florist business Black Flowers, and her subsequent divorce. Police reported that an initial search of Mrs Garbrandt's property found occult literature and satanic paraphernalia. In addition, the reinforced wire used in the attack is thought to be connected to two ongoing murder cases.

Prunella Smyth, 56, described the terrifying attack. 'I knew she was dangerous, but we hadn't seen her for months, not since the restraining order came through. I've never been a violent person, but I had to defend myself.'

According to police, Garbrandt is now the prime suspect in two recent brutal murders. The description provided by Mrs Smyth and implements found match the method employed to decapitate elderly Cornwall residents Daphne Godbeer and Colonel Timothy Manhope.

Henry Winston, Chief Inspector of the Devon and Cornwall Police, issued the following statement: 'Due to the violent nature of the attacks, the investigation had been focused on male suspects, but we are pleased to announce the search for the killer is now at an end. No charges will be brought against Mrs Smyth, who acted in self-defence and notified the police immediately.'

Mrs Garbrandt, 43, is survived by her ex-husband Francis and her young son Charles.

# The Feature Race

*First published in Fictive Dream*

The boy leans down and peers into our car, all wild hair and ragged trousers. *'Allí al fondo,'* he says, waving his arm in no particular direction. His eyes are locked on mine to make sure I'm listening. When he's sure that he has my undivided attention he slowly places a finger to his lips, a secret.

I nod once, eyes closed, not sure what I'm agreeing to. I press the accelerator and the old car lurches back into action, disturbing the dust on the ground. The bottle is under the seat somewhere. When I find it, I take my hands off the wheel to unscrew the cap and take a swig, throwing my head back. My lips draw into a snarl. Last night was another late one, a cacophony of blaring music and breaking glass. I'd fended off the usual questions — no, I'm not from Mexico, but yes I live here. I'll smooth things over later with Miguel and pay my tab. Lou snatches the bottle from my hand before I can take another mouthful.

'Let's try to get there in one piece, shall we?'

I smile, but getting caught in the act always hurts. I try to gauge her mood. She just looks straight ahead, feeling for the radio volume knob. The voice on the radio drones away and we drive past another agave field that looks like it hasn't changed in the last seventy years.

Our little green Beetle struggles along and I give her some revs. I seem to spend half my life in the mechanic's workshop, paying for some new part to keep her moving. When we reach the brow of the hill we see the track — a quarter mile of raw earth gouged out by some borrowed tractor. We carry on down the dirt track and the tattered red tent Eder mentioned comes into view. A few people are already buzzing around it.

We sit in the car listening to the distorted voice of the announcer over the P.A. system, summoning up the courage to face the heat. I push the door open and start to weave my way through the line of battered pickup trucks.

An elderly man in a dirty shirt touches Lou's arm. 'Hello my friends . . . ay . . . lady, lady. Where you go?'

Lou tries to ignore him, but I see her scrunch up her nose just a little. With her pale skin, and red curly hair, she sure stands out. She takes a step closer to me.

Last weekend in Miguel's bar, something changed with us. It was like she'd been struggling against the current for so long and finally decided to give up and travel the easy route downstream. She needs an experienced hand, someone who knows how to survive here. She'd ended things with Eder a few weeks ago, and he didn't take it well. Mexican men always turned every little detail into a drama. Anyway, if she wants more than ponytail and a beaten-up Volkswagen she's made the wrong choice.

In the tent, the beers swim around in a plastic tub along with a huge block of ice. After I pay, I reach in and pull out a cold one, putting it against my pounding forehead. I take small sips not wanting to drink too fast.

Across the track, a group of sweaty teenagers sway about to the piercing *banda* music. None of them are old enough to grow a beard, but they're old enough to be carrying.

I study two men strutting up and down the track, making their inspection. They step over the finish tape, tapping the ground expertly. The older one is about fifty and wears a canvas back brace, holding his belly in position. His friend is tall, with a hat big enough to provide shade for both of them.

When the horses are led down the track, it takes an age to get them into the makeshift stalls. We all squint to see the start. It's *El Negro* on the left against *El Gigante* on the right, a two-horse sprint. The commentator's voice blares away on the speaker as they churn up the track, and then it's over.

'Who won?' I didn't get a good look.

'I'm not sure,' she says. 'The black one I think.'

Lou goes in search of toilets and I go in search of a stronger drink.

Back at the car I take a mouthful of *mezcal* from the bottle and spit it out on the ground. I left it on the passenger seat and it's hot and fetid. The spiky plant printed on the front of the bottle smiles up at me, like it just played a masterful practical joke.

Under the cover of the tent I ask the announcer how the betting works.

'*Uno contra uno.*' He shrugs, motioning a handshake between gamblers. I offer up a bet of 500 pesos on the next race but nobody takes the bait. Maybe they know something I don't.

The horses have the same kinds of names L.A. gangsters paint on their cars — *El Diablo, El Tiburón Veloz, La Venganza*. My pick wins by more than four lengths and I kick myself for not putting up a smaller bet. Just then, my mobile vibrates.

'Eder, is that you?' I say.

'Yes, I juz arrive. Where you guys at?'

'We're in the tent. I'll see you in a minute.'

The silver Land Rover is parked next to the track and I watch him jump out and check on his animal in the trailer. A teenager emerges in jeans, boots and a sleeveless padded jacket: the jockey. His parents are wearing their Sunday best. They helped me when I first arrived in this dusty mountain town and I was grateful. No number, no address, I asked for *Casa de Nila*, and the taxi driver knew where I meant.

I feel Lou's hand slip into mine as she returns. She holds it tight while I speak with a stranger, as if the physical connection will help her understand the language better. I look down at the race card in my hand, there's nothing apart from the name, owner and distance.

'*El Fuerte*,' I say, pointing at the paper.

His eyes light up and his hand shoots out ready, '*¿Mil pesos?*'

I manage to talk him down to 500.

When the race starts, *El Fuerte* stumbles out of the gate losing ground, the rider holds on as his charge veers from left to right. The crowd are up, shouting and swearing. A few seconds more and he's galloping smoothly. He reels in his adversary yard by yard. Will it be too late? He makes it, just, thundering through the line, barely stopping in time before the end of the track.

Two minutes later, the 'inspectors' reluctantly hand over the cash to a couple of punters. The fat one with the brace spits onto the dirt. '*La puta madre'*. The *coyotes* always gamble big, but the house doesn't always win here. The man I bet against sidles over and eventually offers my money. It takes me five minutes to get rid of him as he tries to recoup his losses on the next race. I feel rude leaving his outstretched hand unshaken.

I feel a tap on my shoulder. 'You won? Congratulations!'

Eder doesn't look like the average rancher. He's got a smart polo shirt, and a smart side parting. He walks straight backed, confident, but with a slight limp, the legacy of a previous fall.

'Thanks buddy, I'm five hundred pesos better off, but probably not for long. Do you want a beer?'

'Maybe h'after.'

'How are you feeling? Confident?'

He shifts off his bad leg. 'Yeah, he got a great chance. You know he win the last four?'

'Well, if you say he's worth a bet.'

Lou leans in to greet Eder with a kiss on the cheek and his air of serenity is broken. He seems embarrassed and scans the racecourse. I wonder if it would be kinder to tell him that we're together now. She's bet on someone past his racing prime. Hopefully he'll get another win and we can all laugh about this later. I let him focus on the task at hand and we wander back toward the old tent.

The old woman behind the plastic tub passes me two more cans and holds out her leathery hand for the money. '*Dos Coronas, güero,*' she offers with a smile.

I trot over to the announcer, hand around my wallet. He grins as I hand over a thousand pesos, to back Eder's horse. Lou put up half of it.

'*¿Mil pesos contra El Cuervo, alguien?*' he shouts into the microphone.

The bet is covered by a greasy haired man. A thin moustache hovers on his lip looking like it could fall off the cliff at any moment. He squeezes his son's shoulder and chews his gum open mouthed.

'Where are you guys from?' his kid asks. The boy's enormous black t-shirt reaches his knees.

'We're from England,' Lou replies smiling kindly, 'But we live here now. Your English is excellent.'

The kid looks offended. 'I go to school in Texas', he says. 'I'm just back for vacation.'

'Oh right . . . Okay. Sorry.'

Eder's brother is leading *El Cuervo* toward the start, the animal's black coat glistening. The horse looks steady, even graceful. His blinkers shade the sun and block out the ungainly mottled brown horse to his right. The jockeys mount and coax the horses up to the start line. Eder's family stand in a circle, holding hands, praying. They've put up the fifteen thousand prize money for the feature race themselves.

The gates spring open and the horses shoot forward onto the reddish dirt. They both get out well and there's nothing between them. Riding high, the jockeys look like they could topple forward over the neck at any moment. They grit their teeth and wait to apply the whip.

Suddenly *El Cuervo* veers left, lurching toward the side of the lane and the jockey fights to keep him on course. At 100 yards he's a length behind. I steal a glance at Eder, who watches through narrowed eyes.

The jockey beats down hard on the left haunch and *El Cuervo* responds, straightening up and closing the gap. It's close now, but he's not running smoothly. The brown horse in the right lane canons down the track and remains ahead at 200 yards.

The roar of the crowd fades as I try to focus through the mix of bright sun, cold beer and hot *mezcal*. Lou grips my hand a little tighter with each whip applied by the jockeys. The horses quicken, hovering above the ground. We look at each other in hope, but as they cross the line he's still a neck behind.

Across the track Eder closes his eyes and hangs his head. His brother throws his race card to the floor. A long minute passes. Soon, the noise will die down, the money will change hands and the music will start up again, but in this moment we stand in silence. I open the beer intended for celebration. It's warm.

After a respectful amount of time, I head over to the family, offering a smile. *'Lo siento mucho.'*

Eder sighs, his eyes a watery brown. 'I think the horse got a problem with his tendon because he's not walking so good.'

'Sorry man . . . he'll be back I'm sure,' I say, even though I'm not so sure.

Lou embraces our friend, and for a moment we are all together, like an older couple consoling a child at the funeral. I try to gauge how upset he is.

Finally, Lou breaks the ice. 'You owe me five hundred pesos,' she whispers with a smile. He's not sure if she's joking or not but he laughs. She's always had the knack of making people think they owe her something.

The last race is cancelled. It doesn't matter, the crowd seem satisfied enough for the day. We follow the line of pickup trucks back into town and as we pass the point where the boy gave us directions, she turns her head toward mine and raises a finger up to her lips. I smile and we drive on.

# The Monday Night Club

*Shortlisted for the To Hull & Back 2018 competition*

*First published in The Fiction Pool*

*A university professor, a gay rights activist, a sewage farmer's secretary, a sailor, a pensioner and a barmaid, walk into a bar. This is not a joke.*

Although most of us were desperate for a drink, our twelve-step program was not Alcoholics Anonymous, but instead a three month course: *The Art of Writing Creatively*. Back in the very first lesson, they had stressed the importance of avoiding adverbs, which was clearly lost on whoever named the bloody thing.

For us old codgers, one day rolls into the next — you buy a paper, take your pills, and submit several written complaints to the local borough council. Still, I thought I'd encounter more like-minded cantankerous folk at the start of the week, so I settled on a Monday course. As a 75-year-old widower residing in a London studio flat, I needed to find an outlet for my grumblings, and the classes were a darned sight cheaper than joining a lawn bowls club.

Rather than studying how to craft stories and beautiful verse, we learned to deflect blows and develop thick skins. By the end of each session, my tongue was sore from being bitten, and while the rest of the group were unpublished writers, they saw themselves as expert critics.

During the course I didn't learn where to appropriately employ the semi colon (in truth; nobody knows), but no matter who I shared my miserable Mondays with, I learned that words need to be chosen with care, and shared with extreme caution.

Before we toddled off to the bar, we had our final session in the classroom. Samuel read from his latest sexually charged diatribe. 'I moaned in unbridled ecstasy as he caressed my inner thigh. The flaming sun blazed through the open window, into my tempestuous heart.'

'Very powerful, Samuel,' the tutor offered. 'Perhaps you might remember that a lot of publications don't accept erotica, though.'

'It's not erotica,' he said. 'You're just shocked it's two men.'

'No, no. Only that it's important to embrace the emotive elements of your writing. Study feelings, not features.'

The tutor, MArcus — a trendy polytechnic literature professor — spoke exclusively in meaningless alliteration. He told us to be less 'literal' and more 'literary', or more 'discursive' and less 'descriptive'. In case you are wondering, it's not a typo. We all called him (em-ay-arcus) behind his back as he let us know at every opportunity that he studied his MAsters at Stanford, under the tutelage of the MAsterful Tobias Wolff.

In all honesty, the others were sick of Samuel's agenda too. His readings transformed the classroom into a Soho dive bar, except it was one without the possibility of guilt-free sex. We watched his t-shirts get tighter every week, stretched over his belly, with his bearded head bobbing on top. He announced in one session that he was in transition from *cub*, to *bear*. I had no idea what this meant, but refrained from asking him if that meant he now shat in the woods.

Samuel was by no means the worst storyteller in the group. Rita, the quick-witted barmaid, treated us to a series of tales about Jack the Ripper's brother, who didn't even murder anyone. Another torturous experience was listening to Executive Assistant Gail's stories. She dictated her pieces with the clarity and precision of someone who expected us to copy it down word for word. I did try to take notes once, but I lost the thread with her list of bizarre character names — Finkel Brunardi, Penelope Skylark, Marmaduke Beaujolais the third.

When I read my poem, the hounds lay ready to pounce, waiting for MArcus to give the first critique.

*. . . A lone passenger*
*My thoughts stuck in neutral.*
*Dashboard lights blinking*
*Some kind of secret message.*
*The engine turning over*
*And out.*

*The belt had tightened and torn in,*
*Your heart, crumpled steel.*
*May you rest in pieces*
*On the hard shoulder of my memory.*

'Was it about the car or an accident?' said MArcus.
For a second, I was lost for words. '. . . The loss of life.'

'You sounded more concerned about the loss of your no-claims bonus, Duncan.'

A few of the others tittered. I closed my notebook in defence.

'I think it's because you mentioned all of the parts of the car,' said Gail, checking her notes and nodding.

Being deaf in one ear often helps me ignore criticism, but I was proud of that poem, I'd spent days tinkering with it, tuning it up.

'It's not a complete write-off,' said Samuel, 'I'm sure you can fix it.'

MArcus looked on, grinning. 'Hey, do you know the last thing to go through Princess Diana's mind?' he asked.

Nobody dared speak.

'. . . The engine,' he said.

An agonising silence followed. We all tried to ignore his raised eyebrows. That was the famous 'sense of humour' he often mentioned.

The classroom was part of a drab adult education complex in Holborn; where theatre shows go to die, and cafés sell falafel burgers for £16.95. They seemed to have a policy of removing anything art-like from the walls, and kept the strip lights at nuclear brightness.

By the evening, all that was left in the cafeteria were sad egg sandwiches and stewed tar coffee. Signs at every table reminded us that the staff would remain vigilant against the introduction of 'outside foodstuffs'. If they did smell something fishy, it was probably the tinned mackerel that I ate in the foyer each week.

Gail's detailing of the dark arts of waste-water disposal never helped whet the appetite anyway. She informed us that '*sewage* is the unprocessed household discharge, and *sewerage* is the system of distribution and filtration networks.' Her sensible 1980s suit played foil to a blouse that looked like a tossed salad, and Gail's hair was so wiry it could have removed even the toughest stains from a tray of baked lasagne. Cillit Bang move over.

Back in class, Paddy did his best to help repair my broken ego. 'I liked the bit about the seat belt tightening too hard. It's obviously a poem about a person. Do you really think it is an ode to a Volkswagen Golf?'

Good old Paddy. He was another fascinating regular, an aspiring playwright who spent six months of the year transporting leathery millionaires around in their oversized bathtubs, and the other six twiddling his thumbs and presumably eating spinach. He had a handsome face, ruined by a nose that looked like it belonged to a roast dinner. Sometimes I felt like we were the only ones trying to keep the classes afloat, bailing out water while everyone else continued to pick holes.

Rita smiled though her thick layers of make-up. 'It could be Empty *Seat,* like the Spanish car brand,' she said with a wink.

Even I smiled at that one.

After class we walked into 'said bar'; the whole rag-tag bunch. It was a characterless chain pub, which smelled of olive oil and extra-marital guilt. MArcus was doing his best to trap Rita (who was twenty years his junior and way out of his league), in his web of literary cleverisms, talking about the latest anthology he hoped would help his career take off. We all hoped that *he* would take off.

'Who even invited him?' she hissed, coming back from another toilet trip. 'I wish he'd take a hint and go.'

'Join the club,' said Paddy.

'I suppose I already have.'

MArcus oozled his way over to the group, with his smug glass of port and his cashmere jumper.

'So who'd like to sign up for the advanced course?'

'Is that to learn how to write fantastically creatively brilliant stories?' I asked.

No reply.

'Rita, I'd like to speak to you about something,' said MArcus, breaking the silence. 'In private.'

'You can tell me here, it's fine,' she said, clearing the blonde hair from her face.

'It's a scholarship opportunity. Let's go to the bar, come on!'

Rita gripped her chair like a cat avoiding a trip to the vet. The others watched and sipped their drinks.

'Listen, Marcus,' I said. 'I think we know what is going on.'

'Whatever do you mean, Duncan?'

'She's happy with us here. Just leave the girl be.'

He set down his leather briefcase. 'Well who asked you, Granddad?' he muttered.

'Pardon?'

'I don't even know why you bother,' he said. 'I've got my whole writing career ahead of me. You've got ten years, at most.'

No one leapt to my defence that time. The group concentrated very hard on the sipping of their drinks and at studying the decor.

That man needed to be put in his place, and I don't mean back in the fellows' smoking room at The University of the Uninspired. I pulled at his jumper sleeve and took him to one side.

'Granddad has some bad news for you. He's already sold more books than you ever will.'

Nonchalant as ever, he finished the port in his glass. 'What's that?'

'Well, I haven't been completely honest.' I said, laying a hand on his turtleneck. 'My name's not Duncan. It's Dylan. Dylan Bainbridge.'

'What are you talking about?' he scoffed. 'Dylan Bainbridge?'

'Yes, Dylan Bainbridge. Costa Breakthrough Writer last year. Have you heard of *The Long Hard Road?*'

And with that, the student had become the master. It's funny that the identities of most successful authors remain hidden on the inside a book jacket. Nobody cares what you look like, unless you are 'multicultural' or 'sexy', or J.K. Rowling, and I'm certainly none of those things.

He slumped onto a nearby stool. 'But that was a bestseller, half a million copies. Why are y—'

'Oh, the class?' I said. 'Well, established authors can be such tortured souls, it's much better to share your thoughts with real people.'

He looked back at me open-mouthed.

This was the first time that MArcus had been lost for words since 1997 (which, he had boasted, was the only time he'd ever suffered from writer's block). He shut down like a cheap laptop and stood at the bar — his face a blue screen of death. After a few seconds, his self-preservation code kicked in and he snatched his bag and went. He looked like a robot who had forgotten how to walk, bumping into a couple's table and sending their nibbles into complete disarray. MArcus 3000 bleeped some kind of apology and wheeled off.

I had never planned to tear off my mask like some kind of decrepit super hero, but I got more satisfaction from that one moment, than I have from any book signing or awards gala. Does that make me sound callous? Well, a lifetime of nobody listening, followed by everybody hanging on your next 120,000 words can make you a little cynical.

Lying to them all every Monday was the biggest rush I've had since I accidentally stole a Curly Wurly from the newsagent (and that was last century). But, even with my less-than-subtle poetry, I found that I'm good at hiding in plain sight. Reeling off a pack of lies each week and having people believe you isn't all that hard. It's just fiction.

# Why Don't Dinosaurs Live in Scotland?

*First published in Fabula Argentea*

**21st June: Stirling Community Hospital:**
*Kid 1: Why don't dinosaurs live in Scotland?*
*Kid 2: Errm. Maybe they got too old? They probably moved to somewhere hotter, like Spain.*

Amazing isn't it? Have you ever overheard a conversation like this one, where both people keep checking around for eavesdroppers? One where the speakers are trying to unlock the secrets of the world like computer game cheat codes?

They're around us every day. I hear 'em all. Nae word of a lie. It's because I pay attention to people that most other adults think are stupid and silly. I'm talking about children's discussions — not like the show on the telly 'Kids Say the Funniest Things', I mean the moments when boring grown ups aren't around.

I'm nae supposed to keep secrets from Mum, or from Mr. Robertson, ma' counsellor, but I write down the interesting things I hear and read them back every night. It's personal. Sometimes I add in the things that I would say if I was allowed to make friends with them. It probably seems odd, a grown man paying so much attention to the wee ones, but I miss having a social life. I'm all alone. I'm 32 next month, and since the accident, it's only me and Mum.

Most of the stuff people talk about on TV dinnae interest me — the national debt, which foods have too much oil, the crisis in Yemen (wherever that is). It's just a big worry. I dinnae care if the rest of them on the estate call me Jilted Johnny, and say I deserve what happened to me. Children dinnae judge you. So, I'll stick to what I like. I prefer watching school programs, learning about things like the planets and the dinosaurs.

### 30th May: Arnold Cross Newsagent.
*'Do yous want one?' says the freckly one.*

*It could be the first time they share without anyone telling them to. His older sister tells him penny sweets are for babies and that she's saving up for a magazine. That wasn't very nice. I'd share money with him if I had any, but Mum keeps the money.*

Kids always talk about subjects I can recognise straight away. It's like being an expert for once, an older brother. Their lives aren't complicated like the rest of the world. These days Mum has to help me with even the simplest things, like remembering to flush the bog after I go. I never was the cleverest, but the accident has made me worse. I forget things, and Mum disnae like me going out alone. She's always worrying about me next CT scan, or that the government wants to take ma' disability cheque away. It must be hard for her to look after me; I weigh three times what she does.

There's a lot of concrete steps up to our flat because the lift is usually broken. She had to pay for a sit-down bath, 'cause the doctors said I might fall down and bang me head. That's the last thing I need after the accident put me in a coma.

The park is busy today. It's cold and I forgot to bring gloves with me. I've taken ma notebook and gone out for a bit of freedom while Mum's at Morrisons. I cannae drive any more. Not after the policemen took away ma' licence. I don't remember doing anything wrong. Anyway, Mum's taken the car. There's no need for her to panic though, I'm nae talking to anyone. That's what gets me in trouble, like last time when the park warden said I was using inappropriate language. I said he was inappropriate and pushed the tosser over. Mum had to talk the policeman out of charging me. 'He's been through a lot,' she said. 'Brain trauma is a terrible affliction.' I'll stay out of trouble this time, just sitting and listening, and looking through ma' notebook.

Most of the entries dinnae make sense to other people. Ma' writing isn't exactly legible, but I know what the little ones are thinking; how they are trying to understand the things around them. It's not that different from me, when Mum puts BBC World News on our telly. I dinnae understand a thing, so I just watch the two ticker bars at the bottom of the screen, going different speeds.

### 3rd June: High Street.
*The lady went to buy cigarettes and told the kids not to move. Now they've seen a curly-haired dog.*

*'Shall we see the dog?' asks the smaller one. 'What do ye' say?'*

*'Let's wait for your ma'?' His friend folds his arms.*

*'But the wee doggy is going.'*

*It's risk versus reward. They look at each other, then to the shop, trying to guess how long the mum will be. In the end the bigger one stays and lets his friend stroke the dog.*

I wish we had a dog, a funny curly one. Nobody ever suspects someone with a dog of doing anything wrong. You'd be more successful robbing a bank with a dog, than with a gun.

It's Saturday, so the High Street is quite busy with families rushing to and fro. The old lady sitting next to me asks what I'm writing. Maybe she thinks I'm a reporter from the local paper. When I tell her I'm just writing what the little ones are saying, she frowns and goes back to her magazine. It's not just her, a lot of people think the same — an overweight guy with a windbreaker and a speech impediment. I must be up to no good.

Well, dinnae worry, the accident might have mucked me up, but I'm nae like *that*. Mothers gather in groups, holding umbrellas, ready to hit me in case I try something. They dinnae know what it's like to have no family. The locals dinnae like me neither. 'On your way, Jilted Johnny,' they say. On ma' way where? Where am I supposed to go without any transport or any money? No wonder I get lost so much, I dinnae know where I'm supposed to be going.

Taking out a notebook at the children's playground is worse than bringing a lock knife. The only conversations I get to hear these days, is the gossip about me. *He used to have his own family . . . poor mother . . . never been the same.* Apparently everybody else's privacy is worth more than mine.

Last month, a concerned parent called the police. The officers asked me all kinds of questions about who I was and what I was doing. Now, the benches outside the school where I used to go every day are patrolled. I'd sit there with ma' ice tea (the shop won't sell me booze), then the lollipop lady would glare and the old P.E. coach would shoo me away.

I had an idea how to make some pals. When I was a boy, I used to talk to ma' pals on ham radio. Mum got mine from the attic yesterday. It's big and heavy, and had Cody and Michael written in

Tipp-Ex on the top. Funny, I don't remember who they are, or what their call signs were. When we got it working, nobody tuned in.

Why do some people think they know it all? Yesterday, I was having ma' weekly scan, and the doctors gave all these leaflets to Mum. They wouldn't let me look. Even more stuff I'm not supposed to know about. One thing I do know is I'm nae getting much better.

We're back here, at the hospital, now. I'm reading the National Geographic magazines in the waiting room, next to where they keep the building blocks and toys. It's so bright inside, not like the grey mist outside. There are so many posters on the walls, I dinnae have time to read them all. Mum is talking to the know-it-alls. Now, two little boys came over to play and one picks up a T-Rex figure. It reminds me of something, the two lads and their dinosaur . . . other boys with toys, and a car journey.

### 21st June: Stirling General Hospital
*Kid 1: Why don't dinosaurs live in Scotland?*
*Kid 2: Errm. Maybe they got too old? They probably moved to somewhere hotter, like Spain.*

I know I shouldn't talk to the wee ones, but I cannae resist. 'Eh, yous two. Take a look at this,' I say, finding the page about the meteor strike that killed them all out.

They are interested, and scramble up onto ma' chair to get a better look at the pictures. 'First these big buggers,' I say, pointing to a Diplodocus, 'then the meteor — Boom! Then us.' They laugh at my impressions, and I feel like a teacher rather than a dunce for once. We talk about films, but they haven't seen Jurassic Park. They are too young. We make friends and I tell them about ma' radio call signal. They say their iPad is better.

When Mum comes out, she's got red eyes, and looks tired, like she did when she stopped taking sugar in her tea. There is a man in a suit with a clipboard too. Maybe he's applying for a job. I tell my new pals that's ma' mum and they skittle off back to the toys.

'This magazine has got pages about the meteor that killed all the dinosaurs,' I say.

Mum looks angry. 'Bloody dinosaurs again.' She gets something out of her coat pocket. A family photograph. 'Look at them, Johnny. Remember? Your boys loved dinosaurs.'

I try to feel something, but I'm not a dad.

'They're dead love. Three years and you still can't remember.' She turns to the smart man. 'I can't do this.' Mum holds ma' hand and tells me she cannae look after me anymore. I'm not going to get better. 'We don't know what you're capable of Johnnie. Don't you see? You cannae control yourself.'

'But, I'd never hurt people,' I say, a tear forming. Why am I crying? I hold the photograph, but I dinnae recognize the woman smiling back at me, and the two boys look nothing like my new friends. There's a man who looks like ma' thinner brother. But, I dinnae have a brother.

'Are you still angry because I grabbed the cashier in the supermarket when she laughed?'

She sits down next to me and sighs. 'No, luvvie. Of course not.'

I have an idea. 'Can I invite my new friends to tea?' I say.

The man with the clipboard writes something down and raises his eyebrows at Mum.

Over the next few minutes, Mum explains it's best for everyone if I live at Grange Manor. That's bullshite — it's not best for me. I dinnae even remember discussing it before, but she says we have. I reckon there won't be many interesting conversations there, just more rules.

While we are signing the paperwork, they smile at me, all encouraging, like I'm taking a hard test. I know they're tricking me, like when the boys on the estate took ma' shoes and socks off me.

'I'll get your things from the car, love,' says Mum.

'But how long will I be away for? I dinnae want to miss the Proms in the park.'

'I'll be seeing you soon, love.'

She better come.

I try to remember the last time that I went on holiday without her, but before the accident is just a missing file. Mum goes, and I go with the man to check into ma' new home. It's a bit like a hospital, but no one's family are waiting for them, and there are no National Geographic magazines. The rooms are full, but the corridors are empty. Everything is plain and grey, and the big windows have bars. It's very warm but not in a cosy way. There's nae posters or figures in ma' room. It's drab. A woman comes around with a trolley and gives me dinner on a tray.

I comfort myself by thinking that Mum is coming to visit soon. Everyone is nervous around me, because I'm a stranger. What happened to thinking the best of people and being kind? I dinnae feel dangerous, but the smart man (who is my new counsellor) said I need to be observed and measured. Am I an accident waiting to happen, like a meteor hurtling towards Earth?

During my first night, I wake up with a colossal crash. Nope, I cannae move. I hear silence, then slowly, my ears adjust and I hear the passing sounds of traffic and the hiss of steam. Then far off sirens and a pain in ma' neck. I haul myself upright, clambering out of the bed, breathing heavy. My brain feels foggy. Some ambulance people are talking to me. 'This way please . . . are you on any medication? . . . how much have you had to drink?' I search for a pen; I need to write this down. 'Just lie back,' they say, 'we'll get you straight to Stirling General.'

'But, what about them,' I say. 'I have to . . .'

Looking back I see the car is squashed in half. The paramedic stands with his hands on his hips.

If I can find a pen, I'll write this. It's still dark. My hand scrabbles around on top of the dresser, searching for ma' notebook, then I remember I dinnae have it. It's locked in my top cupboard drawer at home. Without it, I won't remember this dream, or any of the conversations in it. I dinnae know when I'll see it again.

# Carriage No. 4

*First published in Scribble*

Southern Trains, Mainline West, Carriage No. 4
East Croydon, London
Angela Wyatt
15:03

That freak better not come near me. I could smell him from the next carriage, and now he's opening the door. I don't have no cash anyways. Spent my last 60p on a can of Cherry Coke, didn't I?

Benefit barely lasts a week, let alone two, so I don't have none spare to give out to beggars. He's dragging his leg like a sad old dog even though he ain't that old. Pathetic.

Does he think I went all the way to London, to jump through hoops just so I can give this money away? That stupid bitch in the Job Centre is making me apply for the cleaning job I 'expressed interest' in. Why can't people just leave me alone? Just sad.

'Excuse me, miss.'

Is he thick or something? I've got my feet up and my headphones in. I ignore him.

He taps me on the shoulder. 'Excuse me.'

I take one headphone out, minding not to get it caught on my hoop earring. 'What?'

'I need your help.'

He's skinny and unwashed. Probably pisses himself. 'No, mate. I can't 'elp.' I go to put my headphone back in.

He catches my hand. 'It's just, I can't work. Got injured, you see. Afghanistan.' He shows me his poxy sign and points at his gammy leg. Gross. 'I only need a few pounds for a shelter tonight.'

'Oi!' I grab my wrist back. 'Get off me.' I'm ready to smack him if he don't get the hint. 'I ain't got no money for you,' I say, slowing down the sentence, so he can get it through his skull. 'Jog on,' I say, pointing up the train.

He smiles at me, all understanding like, then he hobbles off, taking his little sign with him. You can't let your guard down with men, even for a second. They are always looking to take advantage. Ben's alright, he only gets angry when he's really wound up, but he don't earn much as a mechanic. I'll have to tell him about the baby soon. Maybe I'll do it tonight.


Carriage No. 4
Redhill, Surrey
Glyn Palmerstone
15:15


I straighten out the Telegraph crossword on the empty table and get to work. 1 Down: *Provençal stew*. Hmm.

The sun glares through the window. I consider shielding my head with the paper, but I don't want to look like a wally. It's wonderful to have a seat for once. I could get used to this. Ah, *Cassoulet*, that's it. Sally and I ordered one in that bistro near Nice. Bit rich for my taste.

The trains aren't half bad when you're not packed in like sardines with angry commuters or surly teens. Thankfully, my two are past that stage now, paid up in full, and out the door. I fill in the answer and move on to the more challenging Three Across: *Successful appeal from the bowler* — wicket? No . . . *dismissal.* How's that eh? If only I could tick off my last few years at work so quickly.

I turn my attention to extracting the bottle of fizzy water from my bag, and when I look up some shifty bloke is sitting opposite. He scratches at a burn mark under his lank hair. How did he sit down so quietly? It's a free country I suppose.

I try turning to the Letters to the Editor section to see if I've made it in. I can't concentrate though. The sharp smell of urine burns my nostrils. And here I was enjoying the bloody train for once.

He's got a sad story about the army. Iraq and Afghanistan — invalided out and times are hard. I nod sympathetically and tell him I support our troops. I tell him my old man fought in the war, in North Africa.

Aren't there supposed to be veterans' programs? A safety net, so that squaddies don't end up living under a bridge and bothering people trying to finish their crosswords. He might be in his thirties, it's hard to tell. His skin is so nicotine yellow, he looks as if he belongs in The Simpsons. Poor guy.

'I always buy a poppy in November. Least I can do,' I say, handing over some change. I offer him the water, but he shakes his head.

The soldier acquires his next target and moves up the train, and I finally get back to my crossword. I wonder how many answers I can get done before Three Bridges.


Carriage No. 4
Crawley, West Sussex
Jemima Lyons-Jones
15:29


I need to get started on all of those emails. I'll give him five more minutes playing on the mobile, then it's time to hand it back to mummy. Max is better off without a phone, although that doesn't stop him begging for one every day. Maybe next birthday. Looking at the shapeless grey houses speeding by, I think how happy I am to be out of that cramped two-bed. Good riddance.

I see a tramp shuffling up the train. Oh no. I do try to help, but when you don't have time to listen to the full story, how do you know if they're just trying to pull a fast one? I catch the smell of pigeon muck and mould. Maybe if I just look out of the—

'Pardon me, miss . . .'

Bugger. I should be in the aisle seat. He's right next to Max, fidgeting with something in his tatty jacket. He might be an addict. I can see where he has been bothering his skin. I suddenly wish Justin was with us.

Let's get this over with before Max gets too involved. 'I suppose you need money.' Don't we all. I'm mortgaged up to the bloody eyeballs.

'That's 'bout right, miss. Money for an 'ostel.' He shows me his cardboard sign. Something about being wounded, needing an address to receive his benefit. He'll probably just blow it on drugs. Some people just can't help themselves.

I can't tell you how many cheats I come across in my line of work — headhunting. Imagine what things are like at the bottom of the food chain. I suppose that's why Justin spends fourteen hours a day locked away in a Canary Wharf office; so Max can go to a good school, and not end up limping up and down train carriages, looking for handouts.

Max hands my phone back, the shooting noises still ping-pinging on the screen. Now he's asking the man questions. Oh God.

'Max, darling. Leave the man be.'

'But, Mum . . .'

The beggar squats down to Max's level, sticking his awful skin rash in his face, showing him something. That's it, no more. 'This is our stop,' I say, collecting things as if we need to get off.

The beggar gets the hint and moves along.

Max asks me why I lied. 'We don't live in Crawley anymore,' he says, scrunching up his face.

'Mummy wanted the man to go, darling.'

'But he was going to—'

'You mustn't talk to those kinds of people, Max. They always want something. Just be a good boy and finish your game.' I give back the phone and he looks at it, transfixed. The emails will have to wait.


Carriage No. 4
Crawley, West Sussex
Maximilian Lyons-Jones
15:29


Sergeant Boots goes to square B2, then he can train the infantry in the new battle zone. Two turns until the anti-aircraft guns are

71

ready. I'm going to put them either side of the factories to keep them protected. So close to Level 6.

I'm tapping the screen, moving battalions, building defences, attacking the enemy. Mum doesn't let me have many goes, but I'm not that far behind Marcus and Sandy. I can catch up.

Now a man has started talking to me; to me and Mum. He says he was a soldier, but his green coat is all dirty. I give the phone back to Mum. It's rude not to look when people are speaking. Mum tells Dad off when he is not really listening. He's usually writing emails to China on his phone.

The man looks tired and his face is all puffy. He needs a lie-in like Mum has at the weekend. And he needs a shower. He is more pongy than Michael Parks from school, and *he's* allergic to soap!

'Do you know Michael Parks?' I ask the man.

He doesn't say, but he brings out a sign. He wants money to sleep somewhere. Dad always complains how expensive the hotels are when we go on holiday. Maybe we should give him some money.

'Two tours of duty,' he says, 'and I can't get me hands on me pension without a fixed address. It's not right.'

'You don't look like an army soldier,' I say.

'Don't believe me eh?' He squats down and brings a silver medal with a purple clasp out of his jacket pocket.

'Woah!' It's so shiny. I would love to get a medal. 'How old do you have to be to join the Army?' I ask.

'Max, darling. Leave the man be.'

'But, Mum . . .'

He smiles and I can see that he hasn't been brushing his teeth. 'Corporal Derek Haines at your service, young man.'

I only want to be in the army if I am a Sergeant, like Sergeant Boots.

Mum is getting our things, but it isn't time for our stop.

'This is our stop,' she says to the corporal and we stand up. Mum's being silly. We don't live here anymore.

The man does a salute and walks off wonkily.

She says I shouldn't talk to those types of people and then gives me the phone back. It's got Game Over on the screen. I forgot to pause it. I'll have to start the whole level over again.


Carriage No. 4
Horsham, West Sussex
Alisha Mensah
15:45


I can't wait to get home and pick up my Domino. The fluffy thing must have missed me. Ten days goes so quick, especially with cousins and neighbours to see back home. They all got a story; all want to know how to get a good job like mine. At least the old ladies in Meadowfield House won't have missed me. They probably didn't notice me gone.

I unbutton my jacket. I can't believe it's so hot. Another half hour, and I'll be back on the coast, with a sea breeze and a cup of tea. If I've got the time, I'll take a walk on the beach.

My daydream of ice cream and the view over the water gets interrupted. 'Afternoon there, madam,' says a soft voice.

'What's that, my darling?'

'Could you 'elp me to get enough money together for the night?'

This man needs to be cleaned up. A good strip wash like the ladies in Meadowfield get. And a nice clean set of clothes too. Strange to see someone his age with no place to stay.

'You got no place, my darling?'

'I need a fixed address see, so's I can help me'self,' he says.

He shows me his story written on a piece of cardboard. Heart-breaking, but not surprising, with the cutbacks this government is making. Taking care away from those who need it most.

'Hmm. Let's see.' I take a look in my hand luggage. What have I got to help this man? 'I don't have any change, my darling,' I say. I never carry cash. 'What about this?' I hold up the Toblerone I bought in the airport. It's one of the big ones with lots of baby ones inside it. 'You'd be doing me a favour.' I give him a wink.

He mumbles a thank you and I flash a smile. The smell reminds me of all the dears in Meadowfield who can't control their bladder. So sad. My smile fades as he shows his sign to the other passengers. Honestly, things are worse here than back in Ghana. There's no escape from the suffering.


Carriage No. 4
Billingshurst, West Sussex
Derek Haines
15:55


This is me. Billingshurst. Not long until I'm back in the house, with me feet up and a four pack. Even the 'homeless' need a bit of R&R. The ticket gates should be open. If not, I'll jump the car park fence. I done four hours of work today — two carriages per train and keep your 'ead down on the platforms 'cos of the CCTV. No need to get greedy.

The unnamed soldier is one of me best characters. It were Karly's idea one Remembrance Day. People like the idea of helping you help yourself. I tell 'em I needs a few quid in order to get at the veteran's pension. It's like those Nigerian Prince schemes, pay a little to get a lot. Laughable really, but the public never see through it.

It's all about the fine details: growing your beard wispy, looking hungry, getting an injury that weren't your fault. I soak the jacket in piss every once in awhile too. It kicks off a right smell, but you get used to it.

I can ditch the jacket next week, 'cos I'm switching to Romanian. It's one of me other characters, see? The well intentioned immigrant, abused by the Brexit-brigade. You don't half get a lot of sympathy from the posh types on the train. They need to prove they're open-minded and good-natured. Giving a pound is a small price to pay for believing you're a good person. And every penny I get, stays out of the gypsies' hands, so it's a win-win.

It's not just the looks, neither. You gotta know your backstory to pull on the 'eartstrings. Just like all the contestants off X-Factor. I bought the medal at the car boot for two quid. That was a good one. Got a little boy and his mum right interested, and it nearly worked, but they had to get off.

I do a twenty hour week these days, sometimes on the trains, sometimes in the London stations. I count the money. £68.30 today. Should be more, but I gave a fiver to this little boy in the station. I never give money away usually, but it was a right funny thing, he was the spitting image of yours truly, aged twelve. He didn't say much, but he looked so lost I couldn't ignore him. I must be getting soppy. Even bought him a baguette at Upper Crust. Whatever their story, kids that age shouldn't have to fend for 'emselves. It was hard enough for me, when I was fifteen.

With Karly's dole money, and the extra for the baby, we pull in nearly 30k a year. That's more than the average wage. We just take a little off of everyone. I suppose I could've given him a bit more.

When I look at everyone else, I have to laugh. Would I change this piss-stained anorak for a suit? No way. All those mugs

75

busying themselves in a factory for three-hundred quid a week; taxed by a government who just take, take, take. It ain't worth it.

I get off the train and walk down the platform, shuffling along with the afternoon travellers. I unwrap one of the Toblerone bars that fat African woman gave me, and take a bite. Not bad for a day's work.

Hang on, is that the boy from Victoria station getting off the carriage in front? The one I gave money to? I can't quite make him out. I quicken my pace, forgetting about the limp. A woman on the platform greets him and puts an arm around his shoulder. She's got a bloody headscarf and a bunch of rosemary in her hand. I don't believe it, he can't be a gypsy.

Just as I'm about to catch up, and get a good look at his filthy lying face, his mum takes out a train ticket. The bleedin' barriers are down! She pushes the ticket into the slot and they scurry through. The boy looks back. It's him. I bloody knew it! They turn the corner before I can catch his eye, and then they're gone.

# Sitting House

*First published in The Fiction Pool*

Farouk stared at the gun in front of him on the warehouse floor: an AK-47. He'd never shot anyone before. He'd never wanted to shoot anyone. When he tried to move towards it, his legs didn't work. His linen suit was filthy, caked in dirt and sweat, but his hair was perfect as always.

Things had started so well with Monsieur Belhadj. Farouk organised the parties and looked after the house and cars. Someone had finally given him the chance to help his family and do more than just survive. Now the very man that had cleared his debts, was writhing in pain on the floor, naked, with his hands tied, and Farouk was involved in a mad scramble with a bunch of Armenian thugs. Who said it pays to be loyal?

He touched the prayer beads around his neck. The faces of Layla and his little Fatima pleaded with him to come home in one piece. Only one thing was important now — survival. He reached for the gun.

\*\*\*

It was a warm night in the French Riviera and the guests sat around the patio, in various states of undress. God knows where most of them came from: Film producers, advertisers, wannabe actresses and other hangers-on. Some of them couldn't have been more than seventeen; yet another thing for Farouk to keep an eye on. Empty champagne bottles teetered on the edge of the kidney shaped pool. It's not surprising how many Playboy style parties end in disaster, especially ones with so many drug-addled teenagers.

Farouk moved the bottles to a patch of grass by the fence. Allowing himself a moment, he removed a pocket mirror and checked that his gelled hair hadn't sprung free. He sat on a wooden sun lounger, and unbuttoned his beach shirt, exposing a pot belly.

The mansion was trying hard to be classy, with its designer furniture, white fabric drapes and coloured patio lights, but the building was blocky with too much glass on show. The speakers piped soft electronica into the night air.

Nina came over for the second time that evening.

'I'm bored. Do you know when he's going to arrive?' She wore a sarong and teased her long curls between finger and thumb.

'I don't know, Nina. I am just trying to keep things together this evening and make sure nothing gets broken or stolen . . . or worse.'

'You know your problem?' she said walking her fingers up his smooth chest, 'You are too honest. Hassan wouldn't miss half the stuff in this place. Send some jewellery home or something.'

He drew his shirt together. 'I didn't come here to steal. I just want what's fair.'

She snorted, 'Wake up, Farouk. You'll be waiting your whole life. All these guys are rich because they *don't* play fair.'

'Well, he's always been fair to me. No one else ever gave me anything.' He patted his new Brooks Brothers suit jacket, folded neatly beside him on the chair.

Nina plonked her champagne flute onto the table, nearly breaking it, and dropped into a wicker chair. She was only twenty-three, but she had been on the scene for enough time that the necklaces, the yachts and the expensive dinners didn't thrill her anymore. A mirrored case containing at least five grams of cocaine lay on the table next to her.

Farouk snatched it from her, 'You don't need any more of that.'

Nina smiled patronisingly. 'There's more inside. Only way to get through the evening. I don't feel like posing for more photos or listening to any more bullshit about vineyards.'

How could someone with such grace be so jaded? Farouk sighed and took out his phone. 'I am going to check in with Monsieur.' When he called, he got through to voicemail on all three numbers. What could be taking him so long? Hassan Belhadj liked a grand entrance, but he would never miss his own party, he loved to swoop in and take the credit for an immaculately planned event. Farouk hated festival season. Bargaining with caterers, the trips back and forth to the *hypermarché*, and running the risks of picking up the drugs — all for a few hundred Euros extra.

Nina made her way to the sliding doors, passing a fat producer kissing a skinny young girl. Farouk's radio crackled into life.

'Entrance to patio. Entrance to patio.'

'Yes, go ahead.'

'We've got the police here.'

'What?'

'The police, Monsieur Farouk.'

'Well. If they don't have a warrant, get rid of them!' Maybe they were just fishing for cash again. Like Nina said, Belhadj often cut corners if it meant a quicker solution to a business deal. He had pissed a lot of people off.

'They say they need to speak to someone about Monsieur Belhadj. He might be in danger.'

Farouk looked around, as if trying to locate his boss. 'I'll be there in a second. Don't let them in for God's sake.'

'Copy that.'

He grabbed his jacket off the chair and made his way towards the house.

\*\*\*

Farouk awoke in an empty police cell, lying on the concrete floor. His ribs hurt and his wallet was gone. What time was it? He should have given them more information, or made something up.

He got to his feet and banged on the door with his fist, 'Let me out of here, you scum!' With no identification, the new terrorism laws gave a lot of powers to the police. He knew the score, they didn't even need to charge you with anything.

The previous night's interrogation started to come back to him. The officers slapping his face. Why didn't he know where Hassan Belhadj was? What was the exact nature of his relationship with his boss? What did he know about the Petrosyan deal? Whom had Monsieur Belhadj been in contact with? The questions were never ending. He recalled the boots to the ribs only too well.

He heard the tapping of footsteps and a familiar voice. 'You can't keep him locked up in there. This is ridiculous.'

Farouk strained to hear through the door.

'Take your shitting hands off me.' It was Nina. 'Do I need to call my lawyer, or are you going to release him? You don't want another inquiry. He's the house sitter for fuck's sake.'

There was a long pause, then the shuffling of feet and low mutterings. The bolt slid back and the cell door swung open. The sharp-nosed detective with the thin moustache entered. He pointed at the open door.

Farouk smiled back at him. 'Scum.'

The policeman stepped closer. 'Don't push your fucking luck, *café crème*.' Even through gritted teeth, Farouk could smell his stale breath.

They walked through the corridors to the front desk, with the detective exactly one pace behind. The uniformed receptionist slid an envelope with his belongings over the desk to him. It contained the keys to his basement room, his phone, a leather wallet, a small family photo and his wooden necklace.

Nina waited at the far end of the reception, filing her nails. 'There you are. Let's get out of this shithole.'

'What's going on? Have you heard anything? They said he might be in danger.'

'Come on, I'll tell you in the car.' She took out the keys to the Lamborghini and rattled them in front him.

'How long has he been missing?'

'I don't know exactly,' she said. 'Two, three days maybe. He's never out of contact this long.'

They reached the car and Nina unlocked the doors by pressing the button. 'And this Petrosyan guy. It's bad. He's a big deal in Marseilles — runs clubs and girls. That sort of thing.'

Farouk paused. 'The police wanted to know all about him. He's their real target.'

Nina held the door up. 'Please tell me you didn't say anything.'

'I don't *know* anything. First to be accused, and the last to be told. The cops thought I was hiding all sorts of information — that I might be involved in kidnapping and extortion.'

She touched his arm. 'You're not really used to all this stuff. I know.'

'How did he even get mixed up with this Petrosyan?' asked Farouk. 'Let me guess, another unhappy investor in one of the many new film projects.'

'Something like that. Let's just concentrate on finding him.'

Farouk's shoulders sank as the reality of the situation kicked in. 'I'm supposed to be leaving in a month.'

Nina's eyes pleaded. 'He needs you, Farouk, and whatever you think, he does care about you.'

Farouk stood next to the car, overlooking the yachts in the harbour. The breeze carried the familiar smells of salt and leather. 'I'm never going to get out of here,' he said. 'This place is like a luxury toilet bowl, people flushing their money away, and once you're in, you can't ever climb out.' He ducked his head and got into the car.

Nina smiled a tired smile. 'Bakery?' She started the engine. 'Everything's better after a fresh croissant.'

Farouk felt his pocket vibrate. He studied the phone screen, scrolling through the message and consuming every word.

'Well? Who is it?' demanded Nina.

'It's him.'

'What? What does it say? Read it!' Nina stopped the car abruptly without the rear view mirror. She checked her own phone — nothing.

'It's just an address. In Marseilles,' said Farouk.

She snatched the phone from his hand. 'Rue des Garçons 50D, 15th Arrondissement, Marseilles.' The phone buzzed again. A picture. Nina gasped, and closed her eyes.

Farouk took the phone. The photo showed Hassan Belhadj, sat naked against a wall in a dimly lit room. The skin sagged over his pigeon chest and you could make out the cuts and bruises, some bigger than others. The leader of a media empire didn't look as powerful without his oversized gold watch and Cartier sunglasses. The muzzle of an automatic gun pointed to a sign next to him.

*4pm tomorrow. €5 million.*

They both slumped down in their ridiculous race car seats. The passing traffic looked down on the parked yellow Lambo.

'You have to call them back,' she said after a long silence.

'What's the point? It's quite clear,' he said, gazing straight ahead. 'I told him he needs more security.'

'It's not the time to play the blame game. We have got a job to do.' Nina's scrunched her eyes up tight. 'I don't even know if he has that kind of money lying around.'

'They'll kill him, Nina. They'll kill him if we don't pay, or if we get the police involved. These people, they take precautions — no police, no bugs, no tricks. They're pros.'

As they sat at the side of the road with the engine turning over, Farouk thought back to the first time he'd seen the car. He was selling phone chargers at a road junction, not too far from where they were parked. A young businessman had stopped to buy a cable but unlike most people, he had looked him straight in the eye when paying.

'Thank you, my friend, you've saved my life. I'm on two percent.'

'You are welcome, Monsieur. Have a good day.'

'Where are you from, my friend?' the man replied.

'Algiers, Monsieur.'

'Aha, I knew it, I can always tell. My father was Algerian. Just arrived?' He smiled through his gold sunglasses.

'Well, yes. I arrived recently.'

The man turned off his engine and removed his mirrored sunglasses. 'I know what kind of shitheads run these games', he said, holding up the phone cable, 'and I always need people who know how to be in the right place at the right time.'

Farouk stared back in silence.

'Give me a call if you like. We'll set something up, get you a real job.' He handed Farouk a business card.

*Hassan Belhadj, Riviera Drive Productions.*

\*\*\*

The last twenty four hours had been breathless — a manic rush to collect what they could, sell the watches and empty the safety deposit boxes. Nina had just returned from offloading the prized art collection for a rock bottom price to some friends in Nice. The suspected hiding places in the house had yielded nothing. Farouk had even driven to Monte Carlo to cash in all of the casino chips he found in the office. 'We are sorry to hear Monsieur Belhadj will not be requiring these any more. Please have him call us.' Farouk wished he could have called him, just once, to get just a little closer to the five million.

The cash, jewellery and film memorabilia they had scraped together was in the boot of the car. Farouk put his hand to the bridge of his nose to relieve the pressure of his headache. He wore dark circles under his eyes and Nina had aged ten years overnight. Perhaps it was the lack of makeup.

'What's this guy like?' Farouk asked.

'Arman Petrosyan? He's old, about seventy, but he still runs the show. Runs all of the Armenian business in France.'

'He's dealt with these types before.'

'Hassan usually distracts people with big shiny gifts and job titles when he secures the investments,' she said. 'He promised too much this time, took millions.'

'And people who lend millions, have machine guns.'

'I suppose. He told me to keep you out of it, besides, what could you have done? Gone on a killing spree?' Nina turned towards him. 'You can't fix everyone's problems, Farouk.'

'Well *his* problem is *my* problem. I have nothing without this job, and now I have nothing with it. Everything I own is in this car.' Farouk pictured the rosewood box filled with banknotes sitting in the boot. It usually held his father's old Quran and now it lay amongst old film posters and vulgar jewellery.

'How much did we get again?'

'About €1.5m in kind. Tell them it's worth two, including the car.'

Farouk looked at his watch — 3:48 p.m.

'I've got the messages ready. Get the first taxi if they take the deal, and drive like hell if they don't. I'll meet you at Saint Charles station.'

'I've got it, just don't take any stupid risks.' Her eyes shifted around the car. 'Everything is going to be okay.'

'It would be if we could get into his accounts.'

'Just promise them the rest when he is free. He's good for it.'

Farouk imagined the different ways this could go down. He didn't see them setting their prisoner free. They would more likely torture them both before demanding more money. But he had to try. Without his boss, his passage back to Layla and his new business in Algiers would not be possible. After three years of dreams, the new life dangling in front of him, was disappearing.

Nina hugged him. 'We're all counting on you, Farouk.'

'Promise me something.' His hand started to shake.

'What is it?'

'Layla . . . Fatima.' He closed his eyes. 'Promise me you'll get the money back to them.'

Nina remained silent.

'All of this, it can't be for nothing. They have to know that I came here to make things better, not just t—'

'It's alright . . . it's going to be alright.'

They looked straight ahead and watched the street.

The house sitter checked his watch one more time and released the catch allowing the car door to swing up. Nina said something as he hoisted himself out of his seat, but he didn't hear it. He scanned the block and set off towards number 50 Rue de Garçons.

The steel door opened even before Farouk could knock it. A strong hand grabbed him by the collar and pulled him inside. The man thrust Farouk against the wall and checked for weapons. His bulging neck was half covered with a spider's web tattoo. He was short and solid, like he was made out of stone. Farouk opened his mouth to speak but the man flung him by the lapels toward the middle of the warehouse.

The space was empty apart from a few tools on the floor. Hassan Belhadj cowered in the far corner, hands tied, still naked, his thin hair was matted with blood. He shivered and bowed his head to avoid the gaze of his employee. The heavy pointed an AK-47 at Farouk.

Before he had the chance to speak, the white-haired man to his right barked an instruction.

'Leave your money and go.'

'Let him go first.'

'You have all money, yes?'

'We need more time. I could only get half.'

'I told you, I need to access my foreign accounts,' said Belhadj, raising his head. 'There are checks and codes.'

The man holding the gun jammed it into his ribs and he doubled over in pain.

'I tell you never to fuck with Arman Petrosyan, but you no listen,' said the old man, spitting now. 'You give us back all money *now*.'

Farouk interrupted, 'We have half the money, and I'll stay in his place.'

The old man took a second to think, scratching his grey stubble. 'Bring me money.'

Hassan Belhadj looked up at Farouk, his eyes narrowed. Was he trying to say something? Farouk tried to look stoic, reassuring.

He felt for his phone in his pocket, and got ready to hit send on the second message. Suddenly, Belhadj sprang to his feet, barging past the old man. He drove his forehead into the armed man's chin. The gun flew from his hands as he clutched his face and the three men scrambled for position. Belhadj made it to the door, and out into the street.

Farouk looked at the gun lying a few feet in front of him. He'd never shot anyone before. He'd never wanted to shoot anyone, but it was the only possible play here. Hassan Belhadj had given him a chance at freedom. True happiness waited for him back in Algeria.

As he reached for the gun, old man Petrosyan recovered his footing. Lightning quick, he withdrew a silver pistol from his waistband, flicked the safety off, and fired two rapid shots. The first hit Farouk in the shoulder, whipping his body around onto the floor. The second caught him in the back, exactly halfway up. The impact knocked the breath clean out of him, and Farouk lay like a floundering fish on the concrete.

He stared up and saw his wife and daughter, smiling down at him, softening the bright light from above. The pain in his back roared and he fought to take in some air. With his last remaining strength he brought the phone up to his face and sent the message to Nina. *Drive.* He wouldn't be going home, but Farouk had done his job, and that gave him satisfaction. As the light began to fade,

Farouk closed his eyes and smiled back at his family. He reached out toward them.

# A Boot Full of Dreams

*First published in Laurel Magazine*

Janice Cartwright squinted through the clouds, trying to detect the feeble sun. There was still thirty minutes until they opened the gates, plenty of time for the weather to brighten up. She found her reading glasses and flicked through the *Sunday Express*, stopping at the feature on the Greek islands in the travel section. If she sold enough at the boot sale, she might be able to make some inroads on the piles of bills, and escape to where the sun was more than just an anaemic glow.

'What's the goal today, Mum?' asked Barry. 'A hundred quid?'

'Hmm, not likely. People'll probably stay indoors today.'

'S'ppose the mizzle will keep some of them away. Still, boot sale come rain or shine eh? Let's hope for best.'

'Buy in the rain, sell in the sun.' She wagged her finger. 'You never know what you might find here.'

'Usually, bad cafeteria food and a bunch of dopey teenagers,' he replied, looking at the Bradbury College crest on the sports hall.

'Might find something worth a few bob,' she said, thinking of a nice topaz ring she'd picked up at a previous boot sale.

Barry sat in the driver's seat, arms folded. 'Keep your money. Save up for a holiday.'

'You've got to speculate to accumulate, my son. Besides, I'd need to sell the whole bloody house for a holiday.' Janice took off her spectacles and checked her short grey hair in the mirror. She smoothed her suede jacket — not the best choice for a rainy day, but it was what she always wore on Sundays.

The early morning drizzle floated down like a magician's handkerchief, settling on the freshly cut grass. Janice noticed Barry fidgeting, wanting to get back to the kids, and a hearty Sunday breakfast. He usually left once they set up the stall at seven thirty.

'Not sure if this rain is going to ease off. Shall we unpack?'

Janice sighed and reached for the door handle. 'Come on then.'

They set up the trestle table and went about arranging everything into neat little 'starter packs': stamps, postcards and jewellery. There was nothing 'technological' for sale, as Janice put it. Things which needed batteries made the stall look old and dated. Once they were finished, Barry covered the stall with a plastic sheet. Janice wiped the rain from her plastic framed glasses, fiddling with the arm held on with electrical tape.

'Mornin', mornin'.' The voice startled Janice. She hated the early birds — professionals looking to cherry pick the best items before the sale started. They were just cutthroat traders who preyed on little old grandmothers, then flogged the items at a huge mark-up somewhere else next week. They had no interest in the craft, or the history of objects, just the pounds and pence.

Even though Arthur had cashed in his life insurance, and gambled it away, leaving her in debt, Janice never treated the boot sale as a source of income, as a job. She was just happy for her treasures to go to a good home.

'What kind a' toys you got? Any Star Wars?' he said lifting up the plastic sheet.

'Err no, no Star Wars. I'm not really open yet.' She looked over at Barry who got the message.

The man was short, bald and wore a green bomber jacket. 'This silver?' He didn't wait for an answer, and inspected the hallmarks on the tankard.

'That was Dad's wasn't it?' said Barry under his breath.

'It's been years love. Some of the stuff has got to go. Little by little eh?'

'How about a fiver?' The man butted in. 'I know people who'd 'ave this.'

'That's Sheffield silver,' said Janice. 'It's worth five times that, and besides, I want it to go to a collector.'

'Seven?'

'Look, will you give us a minute here, we're not open yet.' She pulled the see-through sheet back over the display.

'Gonna sell it or no?' he said, waving it in front of Barry. 'A tenner, final offer.'

'Listen, mate,' said Barry, 'come back later, it's worth a lot more to us than a measly tenner.'

The trader peaked under the plastic sheet to look at the other items. He snorted and turned to go. 'A tenner's best you're gonna get. Not much else here anyway.'

Janice waited until he was out of earshot. 'Cheeky sod. No bloomin' patience.'

'You stand up for yourself, Mum, and don't let anything of Dad's go so cheap.'

She squeezed his hand.

'I'll be off then,' said Barry, getting his car keys ready.

'Alright, duck. I'll see you and the kids later. About eleven?'

'You bet. Good luck today, and remember, no clutter.'

Janice watched as he got into the people carrier and pulled away, winding his way past the parked cars, back to the entrance gate. She set the tankard down on the table and made some final adjustments to the display. The sun was beginning to peek through the clouds and the rain was easing.

By ten o'clock the sale was in full swing. The traders, the buyers and the 'just lookers' pottered around between the rows of stalls. Janice had sold a few pieces including some Roald Dahl books. The two pounds wasn't much towards the one hundred pound target, but it was worth it to see the little girl's reaction at getting five new stories for the price of two.

'Reckon that's most of the Sunday punters in now,' she said to the man on the pitch next to her — a burly ex-policeman called Reg. 'Not many people come in after ten.'

'Aye, you're not wrong. It's an early riser's game.'

'You a regular here then?'

'I dinnae come every week, but I do like a sale,' he said taking off his hat to reveal thinning orange hair. 'You pick up all sorts of strange things on the force, I'll tell ye'.'

'Did you work in Lincoln, Reg, or did you retire here?'

'I was transferred doon here 'bout fifteen year' ago. No family left in Scotland, apart from ma boy in Perthshire.'

'No wife?'

'Divorced . . . like most good coppers.' He let out a roaring laugh.

'Retired, free and single, eh?' Janice said, taking off her glasses for comic effect.

'Are you flirting with an officer of the law, madam?'

'Well if you lock me up, at least I wouldn't have to deal with those flippin' leccy bills. Gone up fifty percent this year they have.'

He smiled in sympathy.

'Here, you wouldn't mind looking after my stall for half an hour, would you, duck? I want to have a nose around.'

'Aye, sure. A fifty-fifty split, eh?' he said with a wink.

'Ha ha, you just keep an eye out for people with more money than sense.' She touched his arm by way of thanks and headed off around the corner.

She worked her way through the clothes racks, and past the cars selling Warhammer figures and cheap pine furniture. There were loads of experts in records, toys, and jewellery, but if a lifetime watching the Antiques Roadshow had taught her anything, it was that people attach sentimental value to absolute tat, and often miss what's right under their nose. The best stories were of the people who brought in family heirlooms, not to be sold, but because they loved them, and they wanted to share them.

A few of the more serious traders were grouped together in front of their vans.

''Ere missus, sold that tankard yet?'

Janice looked over to see the bald headed man from earlier. 'Err, hello . . . It's Mrs. Cartwright.'

'Right, yeah,' he said, looking back past her, 'Astley Pierce, Pierce & Co.'

She looked at his dusty white van. No company logo. 'Well, Mr. . . . Astley, I had a lady interested at twenty five. She's coming back later.'

'Some people are made of money,' he said. 'Take a look anyway. Anything that tickles ya' fancy, just shout.'

Janice picked up a brass telescope. It was early twentieth century and had a nice weight to it. She looked through the end, but the lens was broken. The stall consisted of Bakelite houseware, Dalton figurines and decorative picture frames. Not bad, although nothing had prices and she wasn't in the mood for a haggling match with a cockney geezer.

'What about these?' She fondled some coins in a patterned wooden box.

'I'll do ya' two for five quid if you like,' he said, with a sharp sniff. 'Can't say fairer than that.'

Janice inspected a few of the pieces. There were a couple of old pennies, but they weren't rare ones. She saw a metal bar which had become detached from the medal it once carried. *Nive* was a Peninsula War battle if Janice remembered correctly. What a shame the medal was missing, although the bar might be worth thirty pounds or so. As she touched the bottom of the box, Janice noticed a small bulge under the lining. She turned away from the stall owner and dug her nails under the material. It was loose in the corner and she managed to extract the coin stuck underneath. Her heart nearly jumped up into her throat when she saw it was the missing medal. Not wanting to give the game away, she rotated back towards Astley on the stall.

'So, what do you say?'

What was the best play here? She couldn't risk him catching sight of the medal. It could have belonged to someone who fought with Nelson or Wellington, a war hero. It might be worth hundreds.

A hunched old man with a walking stick appeared. 'Hello there, Astley old boy, got anything new in today?'

'Alright, Mr. Bingham, how's it going? I've got a pucker walnut card table back 'ere, Art Deco. And this . . .' he motioned to Janice, who still held the box in her hands.

She stiffened, drawing the box closer. 'Alright, I'll take it. How much do you want?'

'Nice box that,' said the old man. 'Rosewood?'

'Seems like it.' Astley held his hand out for the box, without looking at Janice.

She closed the lid and handed it over. 'I'll give you twenty for the lot if you like.'

'The box is worth twenty on its own,' said the old man. 'What's in it?'

She couldn't let Astley see the contents. The medal was on top of the other coins now. 'Just old currency, nothing rare. I want it for my grandson, he's got a book of old coins.'

'What would you give me for it?' Astley asked the man, still ignoring Janice.

'Oh, thirty I would say.'

This man was a stooge, surely. Janice tried to keep her calm. 'Hmm. I don't want to spend more than twenty.' Her heart was racing, this had to be worth the gamble.

'Thirty it is then,' said Astley handing the box toward Mr. Bingham.

Janice sighed. 'Alright, thirty-five. It's his birthday this week and I promised I would get him something collectable.' Janice didn't like lying. Sam's birthday wasn't for months, but sometimes you had to make the most of what you had.

The old man shook his head at Astley. Janice thought she saw him wink back.

'Sold.'

She breathed a sigh of relief and made a big show of counting out the notes and coins for the thirty five.

'Come on love. Tighter than a bloody Jew,' he muttered, just loud enough for her to hear.

Janice would have normally said something, but it wasn't worth it. It was the likes of him that voted for the BNP. He deserved to lose out on the sale of a lifetime.

'Thirty-five there.'

Astley remained poker faced. 'Nice one,' he said snatching the money and stuffing it into his pocket, like a racecourse bookie.

Janice took the box and headed back to her car, trying to keep a normal pace rather than breaking into a skip.

When she returned to the sanctuary of her pitch, she examined the piece in more detail. The medal bar had four clasps — *Pyrenees*, *Nivelle*, *Nive* and *Ortes*, but without a name and rank due to the missing ribbon, she would have to do some detective work to discover its true owner. The silver medal itself was a Military General Service Award, and was in excellent condition. It bore the head of Queen Victoria and the date of 1848. She knew they were issued posthumously for officers in the Napoleonic wars. Janice took out her phone and pressed 1 on speed dial.

'Barry, love?'

'Alright, Mum. We're a bit behind schedule I'm not sur—

'Yes yes, don't worry about that. Listen, I found something.'

'Not another one of those special edition Charles and Diana plates is it?'

'No, don't be silly. I need you to check the value of a Military General Service Medal. 1848. Did you get that?'

'1848? Really. That's a genuine antique. Alright, give me a sec to Google it.'

'It's got four battles on its clasp, but no name.'

While she waited, Janice moved the coin around in her fingers, watching it catch the light.

'Mum?'

'Yes.'

'Are you sure it's real?'

'It looks exactly like the ones I saw down in the Dorset Military Keep.'

'There are a few prices. It depends on who it belonged to, you know. I've got one here on screen, Sotheby's of London . . . sold in a coin auction . . . for twelve grand. Twelve grand, that's amazing! How much did you pay?'

Janice sat down on her deck chair.

'Are you still there?'

' . . . less than fifty quid.'

'I can't wait to tell the kids. Nanna's rich,' said Barry. 'Keep it safe now.'

'Yeah,' she managed, looking for something to wrap the coin in. 'See you soon.'

'Right-o. Bye.'

She had heard the boot sales stories, of course — the mint condition Beatles first presses, or the diamond earrings that someone thought was costume jewellery — but she never thought she would strike it this lucky.

Reg sidled over from the next stall with a steaming paper cup in one hand, and a bacon cob in the other.

'Thanks for looking after the stall,' said Janice. 'Much interest?'

'Everybody keeps asking about that tankard. Nice piece that.'

'Oh that? Yes, my husband got it for his Falklands service. We've got a few others too.'

'A navy man eh?'

'Yes, he's no longer with us unfortunately . . . his heart.'

'I'm sorry to hear that. Must be difficult eh? So young too.' Reg glanced skyward as if looking for Mr. Cartwright.

'Thirty-five years together, and he left me in a right pickle.' She shrugged. 'I'm no spring chicken, but I ain't got me bus pass yet. I going to have to find another job, or sell a lot more of this.'

'I'm sixty-five next year myself.' He smiled reassuringly.

Reg looked older than sixty-five. He had a saggy face and a whisky drinker's nose, but his green eyes were nice. Janice imagined him pounding the pavement in a beige raincoat with a copy of *The Scotsman* tucked under his arm.

'Did you find anything?'

Janice wondered if she could trust him. 'Err . . . well.' Ex-coppers were honest people weren't they? He seemed alright. 'Oh go on then,' she said, 'I've been dying to tell someone.' She drew a deep breath. 'It all started before opening. There was this little bald bloke, a rough type, who was hassling me this morning when I was setting up.'

'Aye . . .'

'And when I was pottering around the stalls and I came to his one.'

'Go on.'

'He didn't have much, but I found this medal buried in a box of old duds.' She held it up for him to see.

'Are ye' a collector?'

'That's the thing, I'm not. But I do remember an episode of Flog It, where they mentioned how the military medal market is on the up. People are going crackers for them, hoarding them, like gold. I suppose it depends who it belonged to, but it's nearly two hundred years old. Sotheby's sold one recently, for a lot.'

'Well I'll be . . .'

'I gave him thirty-five quid for the box. He got me up from twenty.'

'I've got a pal, you know, who could verify it. He used to work on the force.'

'Hmm . . . my son will be coming soon an—'

'No funny business, I promise. He's straight up. I could just ask him some questions over the phone.'

Janice clasped the coin in her hand. 'Mmm. Alright, if it's just a call. I am desperate to know either way, if it's real or not.'

She couldn't get that figure out of her head. Twelve thousand pounds. Her bank account hadn't run into four figures for months. They would probably think it was some kind of mistake. Her mind flashed forward to the white sandy beaches of Greece. She could get a university fund going for the grandkids, or maybe just swap the Sainsbury's Basics for Taste the Difference in her weekly shopping? The opportunities were endless.

Things were winding down by midday at Bradbury College. Most of the sellers were packing up, or at least thinking about it. The woman hadn't come back for the tankard, and Janice was expecting Barry at any moment.

Reg's contact had proved very useful, and after a lengthy phone call, he had confirmed that the piece was genuine. Janice hadn't stopped nattering since. She had told Reg all about her previous finds, her biggest sales, the grandkids, and Arthur's time away at sea.

'Excuse me missus, err Mrs Cartwright was it?' Janice turned to see Astley Pierce of 'Pierce & Co' approaching. 'I need a word about that box.'

Jan's body froze. 'You mean the box of old coins you sold me?'

'Yeah, the box. That's it.'

'Right . . .' she stood there, arms folded, feet planted.

Somehow he knew. How had he found out about the medal?

'I just got off the blower with a friend of mine, coin collector. It was 'im that sold it to me. Said his missus went berserk and wants the box back, it was actually her mum's.'

Janice didn't believe a word of it. The expert that Reg called, must have tattled to Astley. Dodgy antiques traders were always in cahoots.

'But you sold them to me,' said Janice, pointing to the sign at the entrance which said in bold letters, *All sales are final.*

'Anyways, if you wouldn't mind, it's just everything in that box was very important to her.'

'I don't want to give them back. They are for my grandson.'

He moved closer, right up to Jan's table. 'How about I pay you double what you paid. He would be very grateful, see?' Astley scanned the goods on show, looking for the box.

'Sorry, but you can't have them back.'

'Listen, love, you are going to give them back to me for seventy quid, or I can take them back, right?'

Janice looked around for Reg, but he was listening to the radio in his car.

She raised her voice to attract his attention, 'I've already given them to my son, so you can't take them. They're not 'ere'.

'Balls. Don't believe ya,' he said, starting to rifle through the half-packed objects on Jan's stall. 'Where is it?'

'Reg!' Janice shouted at the red Sierra.

'You will give me that medal back, or I'll turn this poxy stall over right now.'

So he *did* know. What a crook. The car door opened and Reg heaved himself out and headed over.

Astley spotted the bags under the table and emptied the contents onto the grass.

'Oi, get your filthy hands off of my stuff,' Janice squawked, but it was too late, he had already tipped the box out of the bag.

'What's the problem here?' Reg said in his best policeman's voice. He was already virtually on top of Astley.

'Just getting my property back,' he said, checking inside the box.

'Whatever it is, you can sling your hook, pal.'

Astley turned to face Reg, who was twenty years his senior, but at least three stones heavier and six inches taller.

'Fuck off, Jock. Stay out of this.' He turned to go with the box under his arm.

Reg's face reddened, 'You give that back, or I'll punch your nose back to bloody Green Street.' His gaze didn't flinch.

'It's just a box, mate.'

'Aye, and you only want it because you know what's in it.'

Something clicked in Astley's mind. 'You're in on it ain't ya? You know 'ow much it's worth.'

'I dinnae know what you're talking about, sonny,' said Reg, still tightly coiled.

Janice reached her hands out for the box. 'Give it me.'

Astley took a step back and kept his eyes on Reg. 'You know my mate, Smithy, the coins geezer, don't you? It was you what called him. Ex-copper he said.'

'Give me that box back,' demanded Janice, louder now.

'I've been waiting ages for a piece like that,' Astley roared, pointing a finger at her, 'And you come in with ya' fucking grandkids routine, trying to pull the wool over me eyes.'

He turned his back on Janice, and stormed off, box in hand, knocking the leg of the table as he went.

Janice's first instinct was to pick up the table. All of her carefully arranged things were now strewn across the damp grass. She struggled past the table and went after her medal.

As Astley was about to turn the corner back towards his van, she caught up to him. She was unsure how to stop him but she had to try. He turned around threatening to shove her away from the box. Janice held herself back and considered her next move. He couldn't hit her, there were people watching.

'He's a thief,' she shouted, looking around for support. 'A common crook.'

The other stall holders averted their gaze, not wanting to get involved. Astley kept walking.

Realising she wasn't going to get anywhere with words, Janice took drastic action. 'No you don't,' she said, and threw herself in front of the man in a badly formed dive. She clattered into his legs and bounced off in a tangle of limbs.

Astley tripped and stumbled to the ground, spilling the box.

Reg caught up to them, puffing. Without a word, he dropped to his knees, and pinned Astley to the ground. 'I'll knock your wee brain out if ye' try anything.'

The owners of the closest stall inched closer, their hands searching for the record button on their mobile phones. Reg was now kneeling on Astley's chest, using all of his sixteen stones to stop him from wriggling free.

Janice got to her feet, and reached down for the box, before brushing the mud off her suede jacket as best she could. When she opened the lid, she found the medal perched on top of all of the other coins, beaming back at her.

Astley lay still, grimacing, holding his ribs. 'Jesus. This is assault.'

Reg let him up and took out his phone. He called the local station. 'Aye, hello Mary, it's Reg here . . .'

'Okay, mate, I get the hint. No need to get the old bill involved.' Astley straightened out his bomber jacket and started back towards his van. After a few steps, he turned to Janice. 'I'll be back later, it's still on my inventory and I'm the legal owner.'

'Hold on there, Mary,' Reg said into his handset. He pointed to Astley. 'You better change your books then pal, or this place will be swarming with police, and it'll be you, not me, going down for assault and robbery.'

Janice took her place next to Reg. 'Sling your hook.'

Reg continued talking to the police secretary, while Astley weighed up his next move.

Janice thought he was going to make another lunge for the box, but he spun around and stormed off, like a teenager who had just been grounded. She signalled to the onlookers that the entertainment was all over.

Reg hung up the phone and rubbed his back. 'I haven't taken anyone doon like that for years.'

'I hope you're alright,' she said. 'I don't know what I would have done without your help.'

'Oh I dunno,' he chuckled, 'You tackle better than half the Scotland rugby team, I think you would have managed alright.'

As they arrived back to their stalls, Janice saw Barry and the grandchildren drive through the gate. They went to work picking up the fallen items and moving the table to make space for the people carrier.

Barry poked his head out of the window. 'Wayhey, come on, give us a look.'

'Hello, love. Hello, boys.'

The kids jumped out of the car, ran straight past their grandma, and started to grab at items from Janice's stall. 'What's this, Nanna?'

'Leave those please, boys.'

'So where is this medal then?' said Barry.

Janice presented the box and opened the lid.

'Woah, is it worth a million pounds?' asked Sam.

Janice smiled. 'Not exactly, but it's very precious. There are only a few of them, and collectors would pay a lot to have it.'

'Isn't your nanna clever?' said Barry. 'I'll take you to the auction house tomorrow if you like.'

'No need to bother, love, Reg said it might be better to wait for a specialist auction down in London. It could be the star attraction.'

'Reg?'

'Lovely chap. He's over there, look. We made quite the team earlier.'

Reg waved from the next stall over.

Barry glanced down at Janice's mud-stained jacket. 'What happened?'

'Oh nothing, just a little accident is all. It's all over now.'

Barry's attention flipped back to making sure the boys didn't pocket any of the goods on show or run off.

'So, what are you going to do with the money?'

'My God. We've not even got it 'ome yet.'

'I reckon it's about time you spent something on yourself, Mum. What about a new TV?'

'Hmm. I suppose a holiday might do.'

'That's the spirit. Dad always wanted to go to Greece, didn't he?'

'Cephalonia. Ever since he read that bloody *Captain Corelli's Mandolin*.'

'Oh yeah.'

'Where's Keffylonia?' asked Sam. 'Is it in Scotland?'

'No my darling. It's farther than Scotland, hotter too.'

'Let's get this stuff packed, shall we?' said Barry, motioning to the boys.

As they started to load the items back into the boot, an elderly lady walked up. She greeted Janice with a nod.

'Hello again. I've come back to see about that silver tankard.'

Janice welcomed her with a warm smile. 'Yes, it's still here, I put it by for you.'

'That's ever so kind. I was worried you might have sold it. Sales were slow today, but I've got the twenty five.' She fished around in her bag for the money. 'My husband you see, he was in the military.'

'Was he really? Mine too,' said Janice.

The lady looked down, and shuffled her feet. Janice had expected a question about his service, but instead, the lady picked up the tankard from the table, looking at it dreamily, remembering. Janice knew that look only too well.

'Here's the money,' the woman finally said.

'You know what, sweetheart? It's yours.'

'Pardon? What do you mean? I can pay,' the lady stammered, setting the tankard down again.

Janice thought of all those Sundays; her with a small glass of white wine, and her late husband with his beer. 'Take it, please. I've had some real luck today, must be Arthur himself smiling down on me. I want you to have it.'

'I couldn't.'

'I insist,' said Janice, thrusting the silver mug into the woman's hands.

She looked at Janice, then at the tankard, then back to Janice. 'I don't know what to say. Thank you so much, it really means—'

'You just take good care of it. Put it on display.'

The ladies shook hands, and Janice saw another piece go to a deserving owner.

The sun had burned off the remaining clouds and it had turned into quite a nice day — not warm, but bright. Still, Greece was where the real sun shone. Janice thought she would get one of those nice white villas, and drink gin and tonics before lunch. After all, she might have someone to invite along now.

# Thanks for the Ride

*First published in Fabula Argentea*

You were a real asshole that morning. It was eight degrees, colder with the wind-chill, and I was standing by the side of the road with my head under the hood, prodding at pieces of the lifeless engine.

I came round and opened the passenger door. 'A little help, Gary?'

You didn't even look up. 'Don't know nothin' about trucks, missy,' you said, then you pulled the door shut like Oscar the Grouch putting the top back on his trash can. You really slammed it.

I pulled up my fleece collar against the cold and set about waving and hollering at traffic to get assistance. That red Ford F150 was everything to me. Devon and Sheri wanted their own wheels or for their mom to get a better ride, but I told them it was a car or college. That shut 'em up for a bit.

The murder capital of Michigan ain't the best place to break down, but people in Flint are not all bad. A truck with a couple of contractors stopped after ten minutes. Mexican fellas. While I peered over their shoulders, they poured in antifreeze and connected jumper cables.

'Gonna need some new spark plugs soon.'

Great, another expense. 'All righty,' I said, my hands burrowed into my pockets. 'Thanks so much fellas. You have a good day now.'

Even though I drove eighty on the 475, we still clocked in ten minutes late at the Tool Assembly. You sat, stone silent, fiddling with the strands on your bolo tie all the way to work. What was the deal with Native Americans and those things? It made you guys look like wannabe Texans. You traced the lines in your face with your bony fingers, thinking about God knows what.

Even after all those years working in an automotive plant, I acted like a damsel in distress as my eighteen-year-old truck coughed and spluttered, dying its slow death. Flint was dying its death too — a faulty circuit board with more lights turned out every year.

Back when we were all still on twelve-hour shifts, the guys watched hockey videos together on their coffee breaks. That place was so noisy you couldn't talk much. Now they check their posts on Craigslist and organize their second jobs before their first work day ends.

At around ten thirty, I got the dreaded tap on the shoulder. 'Lori, please may I see you?'

The boss. Great. It was her style to pick on someone to chew out every morning and today was my turn. 'Yes, Colleen.' I switched off the machine and removed my heavy gloves. I followed her to her office and she closed the blinds.

She sat there in her ridiculous pantsuit like a fat little penguin with too much makeup. 'You know I hate to pull workers off the floor, but I'd like to know why you were late again.'

'Car trouble. My truck's on its last legs, ma'am.'

The automatic air freshener on the corner of the desk hissed and pumped out its sickly-sweet smell. 'You know we've got the employee financing scheme for Chevy trucks. Do you want me to give Don a call, over at the dealership?'

'No thank you,' I said. 'Saving every penny for the kids' college fund.'

'Ooh, yah. I get you,' she said. 'My Raymond is in his senior year at Berkeley. It's costing us a fortune. We had to cut back our vacations.'

What did she know about cutting back? With her husband's income, they must have been on six figures, yet she patted my hand like we were sisters. I was lucky if I saw six *dollars* from DaShawn each month now he had a new family to look after.

'I'll be honest, Lori. We've got to cut shifts but maintain production levels. That's the word from above.'

'I can't take another hours cut, Coleen. Otherwise I gotta take another job.'

She wrinkled her nose. 'Well, we can't have any more lateness. Got it?'

It was an impossible situation, but I wasn't going to kiss her ass. If this is how the company treated employees after twelve years, I dreaded to think what kind of send-off *you* would get after forty.

'Gary might like shorter hours,' I said, thinking of how exhausted you looked after most shifts. 'He gets a ride with me, and he's past retirement age.' Since my pops died, I guess I kind of liked keeping an eye on you, another grouchy old man.

She looked shocked. 'Gary? Why no. You know he's our longest serving guy, and he—'

'He don't talk back much?' I snapped.

'. . . Lori. The rules are quite simple. I'm just here to make sure standards are met.'

She always pretended to feel sorry for me, but I'd heard the comments she made about me never being married, and not going to church like *her* perfect family. My hours got cut a week later.

On the way back to Saginaw, you got out at West Boulevard. Your house was as weathered and tough as you were. I wondered if any of this block had been remodelled this millennium.

'Thanks for the ride,' you said. They were the only words you said all the way home.

'No problem, old timer. See you tomorrow.'

As you got out, my flip phone rang with Devon's number on the caller ID. He used to joke that I must be a drug dealer because of my burner phone and beat-up truck.

'Yo, Mom, are you finished work yet?'

'Yeah, sweetie. I'm still in Flint. What's up?'

While I spoke I watched you shuffle up onto the stoop and smoke a roll-up cigarette. You sat and surveyed the neighborhood like an old Clint Eastwood in that movie. Is that what people did where you came from? Sitting and smoking.

'Our ride from practice bailed. Can you come get me and Mark?'

I sighed. Another detour. 'Sure thing. Might be awhile though.'

I pumped the gas and hoped Sheri wasn't going to hit me with more problems when we got home.

\*\*\*

To be honest, Gary, you were an asshole most mornings: a monosyllabic rock not wanting to be turned over. Were you a deep thinker? If you were, you never shared what was on your mind. Sometimes the silence was a welcome break from the battles with

Sheri and calls from the school about Devon. You never offered me a dime for gas even though I made a point of filling up on the way to work, carefully measuring fifty dollars each time.

Winter turned to summer, missing out what was supposed to come in between. The only way people in Michigan could tell it was spring was because hockey season was over. We went to work every day, driving the highway with me wishing the radio would do more than crackle and spit. And, while I was putting on weight from late night drive-throughs, you got thinner. It looked like the safety belt would snap you in two if we hit something. Your brown lunch bag sat on your lap like a cat, always the same — a pot of beans and plain tortillas. The pack of Marlboro Reds you got through each day probably didn't help your appetite.

In June we hosted the school cookout. It was my turn to smile and to pretend I enjoyed marshalling Devon's hockey team, who were celebrating their first winning season in years. A few parents came to help but they didn't stay long. The dads gave me the thumbs up from behind their beer bottles, and the moms all went snooping around the house. They gave me those patronizing smiles where their eyes say that you're losing and they're winning.

As I had no intention of inviting DaShawn, and I didn't have any time for running around with a new boyfriend, I invited you. I'd let slip in the truck about how I had to make two trips to Costco for the cookout, and you showed some interest. 'Sounds real nice. You know, for the kids.' If anybody needed some ribs and cornbread, it was you. You got a ride to Saginaw with a neighbour who was headed up this way. Probably didn't give *them* any gas money either.

It was a clear day, and you sat on a deck chair behind the grill, hat pulled down to protect you from the sun, as though you were on the bench awaiting judgement. There was a football being tossed around, plastic plates blowing away in the breeze, and two-hundred pound teenagers recording simulated fights on video.

It wasn't too bad. Devon kept his teammates in-line, and helped clearing up after too. As the guests left, they gave the Ford a wide berth as if it were a sick dog. When they were all gone, I found you in the same spot, not able to sit up straight, your hat on the ground. I didn't even know you drank. Anyhow, six beers were too many for a seventy-year-old man. I never saw a guy with such decorum gurgling into a bottle. Sheri was with you, hanging on your every word smoking one of your damned cigarettes.

'What are you two sayin'?' I asked.

You looked up. 'Oh, you know . . . life and such.'

'Gary was telling me about his carvings.' Sheri smiled condescendingly. *She* was an artist too. 'Says nature and the real world is a better teacher than I'd get at art school.'

I sighed. 'Well you're *going* to school.' She's never listened to a single piece of advice I ever gave. 'First I heard that you're an artist, Gary.'

You told us about your carvings and sculptures. I thought you just sat staring at the walls in your house, smoking cigarettes and reading boys' adventure stories.

'I'd love to see your work,' said Sheri.

'Maybe you will, kiddo,' you said. You looked up and smiled at me and although I had no camera, it stayed with me like a photo imprint. You never smiled.

I pulled your drunk ass up and helped you into the truck to drive you back to Flint.

'Devon's coach said this piece of junk's got no more than a year left in it,' you said, during the journey. Then you went to sleep.

\*\*\*

After Coleen cut my shifts, I took up Uber. Driving Uber in Michigan is not fun. What the folks with the fancy iPhones don't know, is that there are two Ubers — one for drivers chasing five stars, with bottled water and compliments, and one for the jobs no one wants. Guess which jobs I got with my battered F150. I had to make up for my reduced hours somehow. Sheri demanded more allowance, the cable provider was gouging us for every dollar they could get, and Devon was trying to eat the state out of peanut butter and jelly. I shouldn't complain. We were happy, but I felt like I was a bodyguard to the family piggy bank, which was constantly under threat from being smashed apart. I even thought about asking you for a back payment for all of the rides to work I'd given. But then I figured a guy who eats beans and crackers didn't have much green to spare.

The Uber jobs were thankless. Fat rednecks loaded the truck with ice machines, farm equipment or their furniture after being kicked to the curb. These fellas sure didn't expect a fortysomething blue-collar mom to arrive in the pickup. And they all had an opinion about the truck.

'Can I get some air?'

'Not unless you want a blast of dusty breeze, buddy,' I replied.

'When d'ya last change that oil on this ol' gal?' Probably not since *I* last got *my* 'oil changed' by Marcus at the warehouse, I thought. *That* was just a one-off.

I did the work, I banked the cash and ignored my awful rating on the app. People from Grand Rapids to Detroit still need their shit hauled.

At least *you* didn't give me a one-star review. After eighteen months of silent journeys you talked a little more on the way to the Tool Assembly. Sometimes you talked about your relatives. I never had the guts to ask why you left your people, just like I never had the guts to pump you for gas money. Anyway, by then, our shifts were out of sync. It was only a few mornings where I'd give you a ride. You would reach out of the window and tap the roof twice to signal 'giddy up'.

One Friday you gave me a little carving. It was a piece of polished bone, exquisitely done. Fine geometric patterns and a landscape scene on the other side.

'It's beautiful, Gary. What does it mean?'

'A vision of the past and of the future,' you said, as if I should have known.

I brought the car to a stop in the parking lot. It breathed a sigh of relief that its morning exertions were over. 'I had no idea you could. It's great. Thank you.'

'Don't mention it. Wanted you to have it,' you said. Then you looked down, tired, like you were glad your exertions were over too.

'How long ya' gonna keep working, Gary? Do you still got debts to pay? Family?'

'I'll be working until the end. Don't see a point of resting after forty years here. My spirit likes the routine.'

'Once my kids are through college, I'm gonna get the hell out of here,' I said. 'Get a new set of wheels and drive.' I felt guilty saying that, like I was cheating on my own truck, running away.

'Cancer's spread to the bones,' you said. 'I got a few months, tops.'

There was a silence, an emptiness. Deep down I had known, but hearing it was still a dagger to the chest. I touched your hand. It was like a worn leather jacket that had been handed down through generations.

'Gary . . . sweetheart. I—'

'Don't you get sentimental now, Lori. Life has been all right to me. I wanted for nothing.' You spoke with a lump in your throat.

113

'Saw plenty of meaning. Mmm hmm.' That was your attitude —
what you get is fair. Only then, sitting together in the parking lot,
did I understand your silences. You didn't say everything that
needed to be said. That was as good as saying it all.

You kissed my cheek. 'Thank you, Lori.' Then you took your
lunch bag, pushed open the passenger door and started walking. I
followed a few paces behind, dragging my feet. When we punched
in, the whirring noises of the factory came to life again and the
stench of cooling fluid filled the air.

\*\*\*

When you stopped coming to work I called in a few times. By
then, you had turned from a wise eagle, to a helpless little bird, one
who couldn't leave the nest. You still had enough gas in you to tell
me to beat it.

'Lori. Quit it. You know I don't want you looking in on me.
Ain't the kind to accept muffin baskets from the guys in the
warehouse.'

But you did have a few requests, so I came every Tuesday
after my shift ended. Herbal remedies from a shop in Saginaw and
boxes of nicotine patches. You showed me your art. It wasn't
possible to keep it under wraps anymore. There were
dreamcatchers in every corner of the room, bone carvings, maps
and calligraphy. They had a raw charm. Your place had this kind
of earthy smell that made it feel authentic. The intricate carvings
looked like pieces to a puzzle that were waiting to be assembled.
Their patterns called my attention so that I had to steal a glance
every few seconds. I snuck a few pictures on my phone and
showed them to Sheri, but photos didn't do 'em justice.

I rearranged the cushions on the tattered sofa and made you a pot of tea. 'You know, I miss our car rides. Such stimulating conversation,' I said. 'The 475 ain't the same without it.'

You laughed so hard you almost coughed up a lung. That was the second time I got a smile out of you.

When you got your breath back, you asked about Sheri and Devon.

'They're doing good. Devon will be a sophomore next year, and Sheri's so grown up.'

You nodded as if you already knew.

'She's been going steady with a college boy from Michigan State. Finds out where she is going in a month. By God, Gary, the paperwork. It's worse than when somebody has an accident at work. I'm almost starting to feel sorry for Colleen.'

You sipped your tea. 'She's cutthroat, that Colleen.'

'Mmm hmm. They're talking about more cuts next year. I best start looking in Saginaw, maybe even Detroit.'

'You got some nice kids, Lori. You got to do what's right for them.'

I never knew if you had any kids. I bet you would have made a decent father. Every guy in the warehouse had given you a different tragic backstory, but you didn't let it bother you.

One Tuesday, you didn't answer the door. I knocked and waited on the little stoop, picturing you smoking in your chair, carving something with your knife. When I tried the door it was open. You knew. Your eyes were closed and you were sitting in a chair, upright, shirt pressed and your best bolo tie hanging loose. I instinctively wanted to straighten it up.

We had never talked about the end, but you were at peace, and I figured that after refusing the drugs, you didn't have too long. A thick papered envelope with my name on it sat patiently in front of you. 'Ah, Gary, you old bastard.' I choked back the tears and picked up the letter.

*Lori,*

*I never felt at home here, but I couldn't go back to the only home I ever had.*

*After my wife's suicide, I had problems. The usual — drink and drugs. The elders thought it best if I was somebody else's problem, so I came to Flint. Then I had to watch this city commit suicide over the last thirty-five years.*

*I had my carving, and the warehouse, which gave me some order. I never looked for someone new, but, don't let me dissuade you. You should get out there on the dating apps on your cellular phone. It would be nice for you to meet a man (and not one of those bozos at the Tool Assembly).*

*All a man needs to find peace is a roof over his head and an appreciation of how small it is in comparison. You would be surprised at what forty years of careful saving gets you. And you know beans are cheap.*

*Give the handicrafts to Sheri. She's going to need plenty of inspiration at college. The $68,000 in the safe deposit box at Flint Community Bank is in your name. Buy yourself a new truck. You deserve it. None of that finance bullcrap.*

*The house is paid off, probably not worth much. Some young types might like it. It'll be a blank canvas after you take out all of my junk. I'm giving some money to the reservation, but half my estate will go into a college fund for Devon and Sheri. I know that's what will bring you peace — a better life for your kids.*

*The books are for you. I suggest quitting one of those jobs so you can read a bit. I've looked through enough stories to know how yours likely ends. These last few years, I got to hear about the struggles that come with your life. You are too good a person to be*

*dragged down by the Colleens of this world. I enjoyed those car*
*journeys, I just ain't the kind of guy to tell you so until I'm gone.*
*Thanks for the ride.*
*Gary.*

I looked around to see that it wasn't part of an elaborate joke.
When I checked your pulse, you were still dead. Your face was
gray and cold. I called the authorities and waited. My head was
swimming with questions, flashing forward and backward. I
slipped the letter into my bag. Then I felt so damned nervous I had
to get out, so I went to wait in the truck.

The evening sun beat down on the hood. I should have been
sad, or happy, or shouted or something, but all I could think about
was how many Uber bookings I was going to have to cancel. I
thought of turning on the air and jammed the keys into the ignition.
It wouldn't start. I wanted to laugh. It was fitting. Try after try, the
engine wouldn't turn over. I rolled down the window to let in some
breeze, then I sat and cried.

# A Friendly Wager

*First published in Carillon Magazine*

'There's no way you'll make that shot.'

Arturo glared back at his cousin José. 'You just stick to your safe little game,' he replied. 'One point at a time like always.'

Arturo examined the lay of the balls on the gravel — his cousin's team were holding two, and the jack was surrounded. This would win the match for them. The only way to dislodge them would be to smash the balls low and hard. It needed to be the perfect shot. The jack was at the end of the track, so Arturo would have to be careful not to miss altogether and toss the ball out of the court. Even if he did hit them, who is to say where the jack would go. He always played an aggressive game, but these types of shots rarely came off in *petanque*. He stood and thought awhile.

José's partner interrupted the action. 'Who wants a refill? It's my turn.'

'Stop trying to put me off, Martín, you old goat. This last throw is important.' Arturo steadied himself, smoothing his trousers and waddling his feet like he was preparing for a title winning putt at Augusta. The three spectators held their breaths.

'The last throw of the dice,' José said, flashing a smile.

'Will you just . . . unbelievable,' managed Arturo.

The others chuckled.

'Maybe we should get refills; it looks like you could use one,' said Miguel.

'You're supposed to be on *my* team,' Arturo shouted. 'Good God!'

Martín offered to help with the drinks. 'We don't want you to put your back out again.'

Play was suspended as the two shorter men shuffled off to the café, with its lottery ticket numbers above the bar and its big juice machine.

It was a warm summer evening and the air was thick with the scent of orange blossom. The cousins stood in the middle of the park square of their Andalucían *pueblo*. It seemed half the town had left their white brick houses to come out that evening.

'He needs help finding his wallet, not carrying the drinks.' Arturo nudged his cousin in his gut.

'Hmm. That's true.' José was studying the balls lying at the other end of the court. 'How's your María doing by the way? Better now?'

'Oh yes, she's driving the grandchildren to the beach today. It's too hot for me there. Besides, the football is on later.'

'God help the other motorists today,' said José, making the sign off the cross.

'Ahh, you're just jealous she still drives.'

'It's surprising she has the energy, after more than forty years with you!'

Arturo took off his cap in mock fury and whacked José with it. They took a seat on the low stone wall.

'Hmm, what about Patricia? She must be due a medal soon.'

'Fiftieth wedding anniversary next year. She's already started planning the party.'

Arturo removed a pack of thin cigars from his pocket. He offered one to José, who nodded, and they set about lighting them.

'Planning already? She's nothing if not meticulous.'

'It's true, Cousin. It's true.'

The two men rested on the wall next to the court, smoking, watching the scenes from the park. Miniature dogs yapped at their owners' heels, and elderly groups ambled along the pathways between the tall palms.

Their partners returned with four small glasses of beer on a tray. They unloaded them onto the plastic table.

Arturo took a sip, wiped his moustache and repositioned his flat cap. 'What do you say we make this interesting?'

'A friendly wager, eh?' said José.

The others waited in silence.

'Well, we all know I'm going to make it. Knock your two out I mean.' He motioned an explosion. *Bang.*

'And Penelope Cruz is going to come over and give me a back massage later,' said José.

Miguel and Martín tittered.

'Well, put your money where your mouth is then,' said Arturo.

Their partners shuffled backwards, edging away from the bet.

'If you make it, I'll buy the drinks next Sunday.'

'What kind of a coward's bet is that? You haven't won for over two months.' Arturo flicked some cigar ash on the sand. 'What about for the next month of Sundays. Come on.'

'Alright. I'll buy the whole park a drink if you manage it.'

'Fine, no problem. Loser buys a round for the whole park. Everybody wins.'

'Apart from them usually,' Miguel said, pointing with his thumb.

'Stay out of it, Miguelito.'

'Drinks for the park then!' said José. 'Done.'

'Done!'

The two men shook hands, gripping a little too hard, eyes fixed on each other's.

Arturo stole a glance at the café, trying to estimate how many vermouths and coffees he might be liable for. He paced up and down the throwing line, like an agitated rooster. He did a few practice swings.

José stood with his legs apart, puffing on his cigar and shaking his head. 'Get on with it. These people are getting thirsty.'

Arturo exhaled. He squinted at the group of balls down the court and tossed the ball from one hand to the other.

As he drew his arm back, ready to fire the ball out, they heard a voice.

'Gentlemen. Gentlemen, excuse the interruption.' The café owner looked flushed. 'Don Arturo, I've had a phone call.'

'What is it?' he snapped.

'They just called from the hospital.'

He removed the cigar from his lips and stubbed it out. 'Who? Who called you? What is it?'

'*Señor*, they called to tell me about your wife. She was driving and . . .'

'And what? Is she alright?' He looked ready to strangle the bartender.

'I'm not so sure, she is in the hospital. An accident they said.'

The news hit Arturo like a ten wheel truck. He leaned over and held the wall. Just a moment ago, forty years had seemed like a prison sentence, and now he could barely breathe he was so nervous. Why hadn't he gone with her? She shouldn't be driving at her age. The heavy ball slipped from his grasp and fell onto his foot.

The others put down their glasses and approached their friend. Arturo brought his foot up onto the wall and rubbed it with his hand. 'Well, who was—? What was—?'

'Which hospital is it?' said José, after a moment of silence.

'Err . . . The public hospital over in Lucena.'

Arturo took shallow breaths, still supporting himself on the wall.

'I'm so sorry, they didn't give me much information, but I pray that she is alright. Please, go now.'

'Yes, yes. Let's go. To hell with the game. We can take your car,' said José to Miguel.

'*Vamanos ya.*'

The four men rushed off, as fast as their stiff legs would carry them, leaving behind the cigars, the beers, two cardigans and the set of balls.

The café owner watched them leave, and when they were out of sight, he sighed a long sigh. He collected the cardigans, cleared the table and looked down the *petanque* court at the wall of metal balls protecting the little yellow jack. He picked up the loose ball at his end of the court and tossed it high towards the end of the sand. As he turned and picked up the drinks tray, he heard the ball crash down on top of the others.

# The Diary of Xander H. Robertson

*First published in Scarlet Leaf Review*

**Thursday 15th March**

Everyone needs an excuse for failure, and now I've got mine: my parents. Mother has her head buried in charity work and my cabinet minister father has just committed suicide. You've probably heard about it.

You're making me write this as part of the treatment. Counselling. Forgive my scepticism, but did talking things over ever get us anywhere? Uncle Joe and FDR 'talked things over' at Yalta, and that led to forty-five years of Cold War. I'm used to processing wit and sarcasm, not death.

Isn't it *un petit peu ironique* that our sessions are being paid for by the dead man? My student loan goes toward watery pints and reduced-price microwave pizzas, and it's got to last another year after the disaster of the dissertation. Now my personal tutor wants to see your autograph every week to make sure I've been to 'planet beige'. That way I can get back on track with my studies.

It's not just the grades though. I knew the game was up when I stood under the shower for so long that Jenkins resorted to breaking the bathroom door down. Something has to be done to get that image out of my mind — Father, staring through the windscreen at the closed garage door, with the engine running and his seatbelt on.

I picked out this notebook from the Student Union shop. It's not too cumbersome, I don't want to be hanging onto it like a comforter for years to come. It feels strange writing something other than course notes. The lecture halls seem to be full of *faux* working-class heroes with iPads, and Chinese geeks typing things into their watches. Putting thoughts on a page takes time.

It's three a.m. now and I have been lying here for hours replaying everything. It feels like I've got an anvil sitting on my chest. I've been getting about four hours sleep: same as prime Maggie Thatcher. I may as well make use of my extra waking hours and put pen to paper.

Some reprints of Punch and The Strand I'd ordered finally arrived today. The Post Office clerk almost curtsied when she saw the addressee, Lord Alexander H. Robertson Esquire (my little joke). Thinking about it made me smile today. I rather like the title.

**Monday 21st March**
You told me to write about my everyday life, so here it is.

Today I managed to drag myself out of the pit at ten and drank a warm Red Bull on the bus. I was late to a seminar where I feebly pretended to have completed the suggested reading. We won the sports round at the pub quiz last night which meant we got to keep what we could pour in one minute behind the bar. Riggers distracted them by spilling Guinness and I went straight for the top shelf. Classic. We did a good bit of damage.

It was better than Saturday's depressing *Skooldayz* disco. Wearing shorts and a scruffy white shirt felt somehow regressive. I remembered how Marcus Dean used to padlock my briefcase shut, and threaten to punch me if I told.

'Forgotten your work again, Robertson?'

'Yes Sir, sorry Sir.'

I'm twenty-two and I still get bullied, but now it's for suggesting that we should pay less tax. A group of freshers in the queue wouldn't shut up about the NHS being 'torn to shreds'. The old man didn't give thirty years to the party so I could be insulted by a bunch of political tadpoles. I left before the disco even started.

We discussed the 1906 Liberal Party campaign in the seminar. Elections were a lot simpler when you just had to think up a couple of good poster slogans. The professor started to talk about how the term 'Liberal' has become so negative in today's society. I don't think his teaching style could be described as *laissez faire*. He certainly didn't like it when I pointed out that the party had only ever been successful when fighting *against* something and went into a huge rant about Gladstone's four terms as PM. I suspected he was wearing a yellow rosette under his blazer.

Afterwards, Jenkins and Riggers accompanied me to the cafeteria where I stuffed down a baked potato with prawns and then proceeded to lose £6 to the quiz machine. Sending good money after bad into these ruddy lie-boxes is just about the most routine event of my week.

After lunch I had some reading to get through so I headed over to the library. Two coffees and a few chapters later and I nearly missed the last bus home! I normally lock myself in one of the quiet audio-visual rooms which house the archived cassettes and VHS players. I sometimes feel that I was born two or three generations too late. Luckily I made it back for Question Time. The British public's lack of understanding of tax credits supplies me with more entertainment than a hundred DVDs ever could.

**Thursday 31st March**

9:08 p.m. — In less than three hours I'll be the April's fool. Not even a note from you could get me out of this one. I've got to submit two thousand words on whether the Great War or the Suffragette movement was more influential in extending the vote to women. After my third visit to The Spectator website hoping for something to raise a titter, I've decided to procrastinate offline by writing.

10:30 p.m. — Opening another bottle of wine was either ingenious or idiotic, either way I need some liquid fortitude in order to read up about war atrocities and frumpy women.

10:32 p.m. — Found more videos to browse online including an interesting documentary on the invention of bodyline bowling.

11:59 p.m. — If I write this very slowly . . . it'll be Friday.

12:17 a.m. — The second bottle is long gone. Now I've switched to coffee and I am reading furiously, trying to ignore the loud computer gunshots and grunts coming from Jenkins's filthy den.

1:50 a.m. — I've decided that this would be an opportune moment to look up information on Victorian workhouse conditions for a story I've started. The essay will write itself, *real art* must be squeezed out like juice, then the sugar added, then the really clever stuff (you know the *compressed xanthan starch* and *riboflavin*).

3:31 a.m. — Six hours to deadline. Plan nailed and passages highlighted, time for forty winks.

7:38 a.m. - Woke up to a blank page and an empty bottle full of fag ends.

10:45 a.m. - I cained the essay. 1,850 words in two hours. I missed the bus so it was submitted late, maybe they'll give me a break for only just missing the deadline. It doesn't really matter how long we all spend writing essays, we'll all get similar marks. Last time I tried hard I ended up with sixty-nine percent and that's a 2:1, the same as a sixty. We all learn to play the system to our advantage. And now to sleep.

**Monday 18th April**
It's been a little while since we spoke because of the end of term. I spent Easter at home, only it wasn't the home I remember. It was like being stuck in no man's land, surrounded by silent footsteps and barbed wire insults. Jesus, it was depressing, shuffling around waiting for the bombs to drop; only they didn't. We're not very good at communicating, even though all that politicians do is talk.

Easter was especially wet and dreary this year, no matter how high we turned up the heating, or how many fires we lit, we couldn't get the damned draft out of the place. I think the cottage has gotten too big for my mother. She is hardly ever there now that she's redoubled her efforts with her campaigning. She needs a cause, but I don't want to be the one to tell her she should face up to the clogged gutters. I said that if she wanted a job she could read up on 17th century tax law for me but she didn't seem impressed.

I spent most nights knocking back cheap scotch in the Cocked Hat, receiving heartfelt slaps on the back from concerned constituents.

'Any ideas what field you might go into, Alexander old boy?' The Brigadier always was a supporter of Dad's.

'I hate politicians as much as the next man but I have already got a taste for whisky and lies,' I said looking into the glass. They didn't laugh.

I even spent every day walking in his shoes (his wellies actually). I enjoyed taking Teddy out into the woods. Every time he dropped the ball back at my feet, all slobbery, he looked at me like he wanted to ask me a question. *Where is he? Why did he do it?*

**Friday 22nd April**

Got inspired on the loo yesterday reading about a chap who writes to companies about trifling matters hoping to bore them to tears. Thought I would do the same to get my own back on the smarmy Geoffrey in the estate agent's office. He barely looked at us when we came to complain about the boiler and it still hasn't been fixed nearly a week later. We've been taking showers at the gym on campus but three quid is rotten value if you're a weed like me and don't use the weight machines.

Estate agents don't care about students, low margins and endless problems to fix. But it was his manner that got my goat, like our time was worth nothing. *Je refuse, monsieur!* I value my time enough to take a break from my punishing West Wing schedule to write a two-page letter to your manager.

You told me that writing could be a good outlet, and it *was* quite cathartic. I'm writing even more these days, I have even dusted off a few story ideas I had in college. Don't worry, I won't be subjecting you to the first draft of *The Peelers vs Mutant Street Urchins* just yet.

Anyway, the letter backfired because it was a little too creative. Now his manager wants to see me to clear the matter up. I should have just sent a flaming turd in a paper bag through the office letterbox like any normal disgruntled customer.

**Sunday 24th April**

I met Sarah at the Wine & Whisky outing, and she was a welcome break from wind-bagging about bouquets and peat levels. Riggers and I always go together, but we soon split up, like a squadron breaking formation peeling off into the dogfight. I am certainly no ladies' man, but I could lie for England, so after a few single malts, turning on the charm isn't too difficult.

You're the only person I can talk to about my relationship for fear of more Twitter screenshots or Daily Mirror *exposés*. I don't care if she scolds me like a naughty schoolboy, I could listen to her for hours. And, when we don't talk, the silences aren't awkward. We met for coffee the next day, and the next day. She's a big reader, (although she didn't seem taken with my time travelling space mutants idea). I haven't had the heart to tell Mum about my budding relationship yet, it might prove too painful for her.

**Monday 2nd May**

Last week I told you how I felt like I was climbing out of the hole that David Robertson MP's death dropped me into. It turns out that it's more of a sea, and the when the tide changes the swell just gets bigger. I spent so long fighting off reporters that when the adrenaline ebbed away, I found myself clinging to my lifeboat of university routine.

I haven't had much desire for parties of late, they always end up with drunken stragglers huddling around some funny internet video. No one wants to put the world to rights, no one wants to talk politics around me.

Today I made up some excuse about a sore throat in order to avoid my 'heavy' schedule of two lectures. Sarah and the books have been keeping me company *dans la maison*, but it's not easy on her with three brutes sharing a kitchen covered in kebab grease and dirty tea cups.

**Friday 6th May**

Success! I submitted a short piece to the student rag and it's going to be published. One of the lads from my school is the assistant editor and he said they normally have plenty of space. It's all about who you know. My first by-line, and all this from a £3.99 notebook. I suppose it will be the first positive piece of Robertson news published in a good while.

I've started going to the writing club every week now. The Lit twits all come in with their coloured woollen scarves and some tatty classic gripped under their arm. They hate me. My brash striped shirts make them want to cower together in the corner. They sniff and snort at my readings, but it feels good to reel something off, like I am shedding a skin and leaving it for all to admire. I don't pay attention to the criticism. At least Sarah liked my Victorian science fiction story. Sometimes a close friend's support is worth more than public opinion.

**Monday 16th May**

Sarah's texts got snarky, then angry, then desperate, and then there were none. Another empty space. Too much time writing and drinking wine alone, apparently. I should never have trusted her to understand. Even though she has exams and I am postponing mine until next year, I can't donate enough of my time.

I've got to think about the summer, and what I'm going to do with myself before I re-enrol for my final year. I'll have to see if I can still take up the internship at the think tank that he organised. That's going to be an awkward conversation.

**Wednesday 18th May**

I traipsed around the careers fair without giving out a single CV: accountant, accountant, actuary, HR, finance, accountant. Why the hell are the brightest graduates so desperate to be locked into a program that guarantees mediocrity? Scarface was wrong. Everyone's got money now, it doesn't get you power, it just gets you deeper into the mire. Before you know it you'll be scrabbling around in the dirt for a ten percent raise while those with the real power smile on and take their cut. Don't we want to prove ourselves as men anymore? My father spent years raising funds and kissing the right arses for his safe seat, but it still wasn't enough for him. He wanted positive change. You asked me about my future last session and the sight of honours students grabbing at free corporate pens on offer made me want change too.

All of my unlucky housemates are burning the midnight oil studying, while I send begging letters to Westminster polling companies asking to work for free for the summer. I think most of them can't see past the potential oil slick of a tabloid headline. Most of them haven't even replied.

**Saturday 4th June**

With my bow tie open around my neck and a red wine glow, I sat at the table taking notes on my peers' antics. Everyone else at the Leavers' Ball was *actually* leaving and I felt trapped in limbo, a purgatory of bad DJs and tacky photo poses. The notes will make a better keepsake.

You told me I'd regret it if I didn't go. I suppose the Union did a good job putting on some decent bands and a TV panel show comedian. My head still feels like it is strapped onto a whirly fairground ride this morning. When can I get off?

**Thursday 9th June**

Today is my final session with you. One final signature and my book is finished. I am even doing my homework and writing this *before* class this time. I must be ready to handle my degree course again (cue your sarcastic eye roll).

I have papered over some of the cracks that appeared after the funeral and I'm back into a routine of walking and writing. The showers are even down to a brief three minutes now, *a la* James Bond. I don't want you to get all cocky about helping the next politician's grieving child, but the diary was a good idea. It's funny how a blank page sometimes makes the best pair of ears.

I talked to the party chairman on the phone this week and he said he could arrange a summer placement and we could talk about a 2020 running date. Xander H. Robertson MP. You heard it here first. Perhaps I'll even make the upper house.

# A Terminal Christmas

*First published in Storgy*

*A terminal Christmas in an unknown city*
*Wishing you had more than baggage to reclaim*
*The queues are comprised of furrowed brows*
*And the tickets invalid for the date today.*

*Thinly veiled fury, of a passenger mob*
*Looking for somewhere to place the blame*
*In an airport terminal at Christmas time*
*Nobody knows your name.*

'Is it a machine gun?' Shari knew it wasn't a machine gun in the case, but it was a good way to break the ice.

Graeme was sitting on the floor with his back resting against a pillar. 'No no. It's drugs. Lots of drugs.'

'Ha ha, right.' Shari smiled, tapping the side of her nose. 'What is it really, a violin?'

He looked around and raised a hand to the opposite side of his mouth. 'Don't tell anyone,' he whispered, 'but it's a ukulele.'

'Okay then,' she whispered back. Were ukuleles that embarrassing, or were they just too popular? 'We're supposed to follow the staff to Baggage Area 1 apparently. I'm Shari by the way.'

'Graeme. Nice to meet you,' he said, standing up in instalments. He towered over her, not knowing whether to go for a kiss on the cheek or not. Eventually, he settled on an awkward handshake.

'Bloody nightmare getting all the way here before they cancelled it,' she said. 'No text, or email or anything. I really needed to get back to London tonight. Somehow my family are going to make all of this *my* fault.'

'Yeah . . . families, eh?'

Shari was pushing thirty, with bright eyes and smooth dark skin. She looked over at a flight attendant handing out paperwork and listening to passengers' complaints. 'What a joke eh? I'm supposed to be going to the theatre with my niece tonight. Panto.'

'. . . Oh no you weren't.'

She sighed, 'Hey, not funny. I'm meeting someone important there.'

'Have you got a date with Peter Pan?'

'I'm meeting a new talent agent *actually*.'

'Oh, you tread the boards, do you?'

She straightened a loose strand of hair, 'Mmm, sort of. I've had a few acting jobs.'

Actually, she'd had more than a few acting jobs: fringe theatre, a recurring role on a soap, and her big break, the role of nurse Sanya Shah on a medical drama. Just her luck that the show had been cancelled six months after she joined, ending an eight year run. Her relationship with Dr. Ross on the show had ended at about the same time too. With no job and no husband, there was sure to be a full investigation when she got home and found various Indian relatives parked on the sofa.

Graeme and Shari trudged down the escalators with the other passengers, past the shops, and back through the passport control. It was like playing a computer game in reverse, going back to level one. They finally came to the deserted baggage hall, with the vending machines standing guard around the perimeter of the room.

'It looks like someone has bought a few too many bottles of brandy.' Graeme pointed at a young redhead with stick thin legs. She was struggling to liberate two large roller bags from the baggage carousel. Shari nodded, already looking around for a baggage trolley for her leather suitcases. Graeme spotted his green backpack and grabbed it in one swift motion. He helped Shari haul her cases onto a trolley.

'Jesus, what's in this one, a complete nativity scene cast in bronze?'

They watched as the others collected their luggage — low cost airline passengers, stranded in Spain on Christmas Eve. Couples stood silent, with arms folded, or jabbed at their phones. Near the customs exit a smartly dressed business woman looked at her watch, tutting every thirty seconds like an angry kitchen timer. The guy next to Shari made bad jokes whilst his wife pretended she wasn't embarrassed. Shari gave him an encouraging glance. Their young daughter with a pudding-basin bob yawned.

After a while, the weary passengers marched outside and boarded the bus, scrambling for the last remaining free double seats.

'Saved you a seat,' Graeme said, and tapped the place next to him.

Shari scooted into the aisle seat and swung her legs over her duty free bag.

'So come on then, I'll bite. What are you doing in Spain on Christmas Eve?' she asked.

'I'm coming back from Colombia. Just flew in today. I've been working there for a while.'

'Ooh, sounds mysterious.'

'Not really, I take whatever work is going, hostel barman, farm work, a bit of web design. The visas run out eventually.'

'Back home to see the family once a year, is that it?'

'Yeah, something like that.'

'My family would go bananas if I didn't come back at Christmas. We've got all of these relatives to show off to. You know, businesses to brag about, and marriages to arrange.'

Graeme looked sheepish. 'Sounds uncomfortable. What about you? Why are you in Spain?'

'Well, now my story's gonna seem pathetic. First I lost my job, then I got dumped, so decided to do a bit of present shopping and stay in a nice hotel. I've spent a shit-load. To be honest, most of the stuff I got was for me.' Shari looked down, 'I shouldn't be spending all the money really, but I've put off thinking about credit cards until January.'

'What about this lot?' he said looking at the other maroonees, 'so many Brits coming back from Madrid on Christmas Eve. I reckon they must be workers or something. Teachers?'

He nodded towards an angular blond wearing a pea coat. 'Definitely a teacher. I bet she gave those airline reps a good telling off.' He put on a high pitched voice, *'I'm going to notify Martin Lewis of the Money Saving Expert team.'*

Shari laughed and leaned back in her seat.

They started to move and she soon drifted into a catatonic state, not really asleep, but not fully aware of the sights of the city passing by. Shops closed their shutters for the holiday, leaving the city in a half-lit dusk. The bus wound its way around the inner highways of Madrid as its prisoners kept a lookout for any recognisable landmarks. All they saw was Motel California, Carrefour, and Bar Tropicana. A ripple of excitement spread as they passed the large neon sign for Hotel Real. Three stars.

'Like they're going to put us up *there*,' Shari murmured.

The bus turned into the hotel drop off point.

'They bloody are.'

The chattering increased.

***

What was taking him so long? The tables were already filling up. Shari tapped her foot praying that the chair next to her wouldn't be filled by another diner. Finally, she saw Graeme emerge from the foyer looking a shade lighter after his shower.

'Ah, there you are,' said Shari. 'I'm Hank Marvin.'

Graeme looked at her quizzically.

'Hank Marvin . . . *starving*. Come on.'

'Right! Well . . . nice to meet you Hank.' He offered his right hand.

When Graeme sat down and they were finally at eye level, Shari caught him admiring her small nose stud.

'Hi there, I'm Samantha.' The pretty girl from the baggage carousel beamed at them from across the table. 'This place is totes amazing, isn't it?' she said looking at the buffet. 'And we've all got our own rooms. It totally makes up for it all.'

She was young, thought Shari, possibly a student. As everybody at the table introduced themselves, she feigned sympathy at their sob stories of how terrible it was to be away from home on Christmas Eve. Shari was glad. She would have felt like a caged animal back in Crawley.

*'How much did you earn in your last job? And how much is unemployment nowadays?'* According to her mother, she only had two years to get married or she would be single forever.

Shari grabbed the wine bottle in the middle of the round table. 'At least they know how to treat a lady here.' She winked at Graeme. He seemed like the only other person who saw the unexpected stopover as a blessing not a curse.

Graeme reached for the bottle as Shari placed it back on the table, 'When in Rome . . . or Spain I should say.' Their hands touched for a brief moment.

The dining room looked like something out of an old wedding video. Red carpet that was a little too dark, high backed chairs with white covers, and plastic flowers on each table. A huge stainless steel buffet station, dominated the room.

The food consisted of the usual bizarre mix of cuisines interspersed with platters of rice and bread in the hope that the guests would fill up on the cheap stuff. The desserts came straight out of the 1970s — *crème caramels*, jellies, and white ice cream with sprinkles.

Shari prodded at her chicken. She didn't trust the herbs swimming around in the sauce. 'Look at 'er royal highness over there,' she said, pointing to a old Spanish lady. The lady wore an olive green jacket with a silk neckerchief. Her grey hair was scraped back into a perfect bun. Shari hoped she wouldn't turn into someone who dressed up to go to a hotel buffet dinner, even if she did end up with that toothy little Indian dentist that her mum was lining up. The thrill of judging people was the oxygen being pumped into the room, keeping everyone alert, despite the tiredness. Shari tore a piece of bread in two so as not to appear too hungry.

Graeme caught the waiter's attention, '*Errr, una botella de vino más por favor?*' he asked rather than ordered. The waiter waltzed off, giving no indication of whether he was going to bring one or not.

'You should learn to beg forgiveness, not ask for permission,' Shari said, pointing at the wine on the empty tables across the room. She got up from her seat and set off on a mission to liberate one.

\*\*\*

Bar Tropicana turned out to be a strip joint. Shari had tried to cajole half the planc into going out but only Graeme, and Samantha the peppy redhead, were game. They had helped themselves to nearly a full bottle of wine each at dinner, and both girls needed to steady themselves on the walk, clutching on Graeme's arms, one either side.

'I don't suppose you girls know anywhere else around here,' he said.

Samantha looked puzzled. 'I'm surprised even this is open. People here take holidays very seriously.'

Graeme looked at his watch — 12:08 AM. 'Let's have a drink anyway, it's Christmas for Christ's sake!'

Shari looked back towards the hotel. The ten minute walk along the dual carriageway was not appealing. A couple of strong cocktails might help her forget about what she'd already spent on the credit card. Ah yes, the card! She might even be able to claim it had been stolen and used in the club.

Samantha hung back, not wanting to pass the heavy-set bouncer guarding the door. He had a floppy Santa hat, but he didn't really look in the spirit of it.

'Come on, drinks are on me.' Shari marched over and dragged Samantha through the entrance. Graeme followed them in obediently, raising his eyebrows to the doorman.

The club was empty. Not even a single dancer. Euro pop pounded the walls, and coloured lights swept from left to right and from floor to ceiling. A huge banner hung above the stage — *Felíz Navidad.*

The hostess showed them the way to a booth and Shari opened her purse and pulled out her credit card. She ordered three mojitos. For once she didn't have to care how much they would be.

Samantha, eyes glazed, stood up to dance in the booth. She showed off her best GoGo moves, raising her arms like a puppet.

Graeme grinned, 'At least someone is putting on a show, it's just us in here.'

The drinks had arrived, all forty-five Euros worth of them. Shari laughed at the bill. Samantha took gulps of hers in between her 1960s dance routines.

'Let's go up there.' Samantha pointed to the empty stage, lights still sweeping side to side.

'Hmm, not my bag, sweetheart. I'll pass.'

'I need a partner, come on.' Now it was Samantha's turn to pull at Shari's wrist.

It felt like a situation from one of those 'choose your own adventure' books she had read as a child.

*Inventory: Gucci heels, two Louis Vuitton suitcases, a cured cheese hamper, Tiffany earrings, a Swarowski crystal iPhone cover, Actors and Performers Yearbook.*

*Money: -£4,500*

*Situation: You sit in a deserted tavern with a chivalrous knight. Do you*
*a) Use bawdy jokes and promiscuous dance to entertain him? Or*
*b) Forge a relationship through cultured conversation?*
  *Turn to page 371 to continue.*

Samantha tried again. 'Don't be a grumpy goose. Come on.'

'Just leave it. For fuck's sake!' Shari finally recovered her arm, and smoothed her wrist with her other hand.

Samantha shrugged, 'Be like that.' She took another gulp of mojito and headed off to the stage.

Samantha writhed up and down against the pole on stage. Shari looked around to see if anyone would stop her. The bouncer, whose head looked like an oversized ball of stuffing had come inside. He just stood there with his arms folded, watching.

'I thought you would have fancied a dance,' shouted Graeme over the music.

'Yeah,' Shari drew her glass closer to her. 'I guess I am still just a bit . . . well, he was seeing a younger woman . . . a redhead actually.'

'Shit, I'm sorry. Were you going out long?'

'No, not really, but you know,' she put on a deep gravelly voice, 'I'm getting too old for this shit.'

'Ha ha. Well, you don't look a day older than you are.'

'I didn't even tell you how old I am!'

'Busted. You got me,' said Graeme putting his hands up. It probably worked sometimes. They both laughed. 'Cheers' he said, raising his glass, 'Merry Christmas'.

He moved in for a kiss on the cheek, but Shari surprised him by turning and meeting him on the lips. She drew him closer and ran a hand through his thick hair. The pumping music around them faded, and she was finally free of everything — the Job Centre, the family questions and the calls from the bank.

On their way back to the hotel, Shari pulled Samantha aside. 'Sorry about that in there. I'm just going through some stuff.'

'What?' Samantha appeared to have forgotten already. 'Don't worry about it.'

The two girls hugged and Samantha lost her balance, almost sending them crashing down to Earth on the side of the motorway.

***

They had been waiting at baggage reclaim for nearly half an hour, after finally touching down in London. The pudding-bowl haircut girl struck up a conversation with a guy who was wearing a cardboard Burger King crown and sunglasses.

'They *have* to switch it on soon.'

'There's probably not even any fucking baggage handlers on today.' He glanced at the girl's parents, 'Oh, yeah, sorry. Excuse the French.'

The mother had tried to covered her daughter's ears, but it was too late.

'Don't worry,' said the girl with the hands still over her ears, 'my mum swears too. And she drinks. *A lot.*'

The Burger King burst into laughter, his eyes hidden behind the dark glasses.

The mum went red and busied herself trying to look through the plastic curtain to see when the bags would arrive.

Samantha turned to Shari, 'So, spill the beans. What did you two get up to after the club then?'

Shari paused, 'Well, he invited me back to his room and . . . ' she checked to see if anyone was eavesdropping, 'you know, we had fun.'

'No way!' Samantha's eyes seemed to glow bright from the new gossip. She rubbed her hands together. 'Exciting'.

'Keep your hair on. It's not exactly wedding bells, just a drunken shag.' It was more like a rebound, but Shari didn't want to bring up Dr. Ross and his redhead again.

'So you don't really like him then?'

Shari looked over at him. 'Graeme's nice, you know. Easy going. He's definitely a lot lower maintenance than the last one. More trustworthy too.'

'Well, it will make a good story, meeting at Club Tropicana.' Her eyes dimmed a little 'Oh God, the dancing. Tell me you didn't take any photos.'

'Your secret is safe with me.' Shari scrunched up her eyes. The light was brighter than in an operating theatre.

'Quick airport selfie?' asked Samantha.

'Sure, if you want.' Shari opened her eyes and put on her best headshot smile. 'Merry Christmas.'

Samantha raised the phone up high and the girls pouted in front of the sterile background. They embraced and said their goodbyes.

Graeme had plonked himself down across the hall and was plucking his ukulele, oblivious to the impatient foot tapping going on around him. Shari wandered over.

Graeme looked up, 'Hello, you.'

'What are you playing, 'Last Christmas' by Wham?'

'No, I'm writing a little song about the greatest pole dancers in Madrid.'

Shari glared at him, but his smile didn't break. She smoothed a loose strand of hair.

He made another note in his little red book and put the instrument down.

'So where are you going for Christmas today? Got something lined up? I'm virtually a stone's throw from my lot, although I wouldn't be surprised if they've given my bed away to some distant cousin already.'

'Hah. No, I don't really bother with Christmas. Haven't been back in years.'

'How come you're back this year?'

'Some friends invited me to stay with them. Out of pity.'

'Where do they live?'

'I don't think I can stomach it — turning up like a little lost boy on Christmas Day. I haven't even told them we've landed yet.'

'You should go. Don't worry about being a third wheel, just go. It's important.'

It was the first time that Graeme had seemed unsure of anything, and Shari thought that although her family was bonkers, it was something to be thankful for. 'Come on, Graeme, who else is going to play Jingle Bells on the ukulele?'

'I'll hang around a bit, see if I can get a last minute deal. Thailand is always nice this time of year.'

'I'd run away with you if I wasn't so broke. I tossed all of my credit cards in the bin after last night. I can't report them stolen just for some bloody mojitos.'

'Good for you. You've got the jump on your New Year's Resolution.'

'Mmm. And what's your resolution? Stop ending up in strip clubs on Christmas Eve?'

'Actually the opposite,' he said, 'need to go more often if I get to meet people like you.'

Shari's heart jumped — the good kind of jump, the kind she hadn't felt for a while. 'That's sweet.'

He leaned down and kissed her on the cheek, and Shari wished that she could take Graeme's hand, jump on the next plane, and explore somewhere new together. But, she had to go back to Crawley and face the music.

'Watch this will you?' said Graeme, pointing at the ukulele, 'I'm going to take a leak.'

Shari waited until he was out of sight and picked up the notebook. Above the lines of scrawled lyrics was a title, underlined — 'A Terminal Christmas'. She picked up the pen lying next to the ukulele and added her name and number under the final line of the song.

Suddenly, the baggage carousel sprang into action. The passengers of flight MA351 jostled for position, straining their eyes to see which black roller bag might be theirs. Shari saw the familiar brown leather her Louis Vuitton case making its way down the line. She found a space and set her feet, ready to pull it off the machine. An old green backpack soon followed down the line of bags, but its owner was nowhere to be seen.

# Out Cold

*First published in Near To The Knuckle*

Marlon couldn't breathe. He grimaced in agony and clamped a hand to his ribs. His opponent's fist had slammed home into its target, flipping the pain level from zero to searing.

He was used to fighting through pain, but for him to be this hurt was rare. Most people don't know how a punch like that can shut down the body; it's what fighters fear the most. Thousands of rounds of hard sparring builds a certain toughness and grit, but nobody is made of stone. That shot could have put down an elephant, let alone an aging hundred-and-seventy pounder.

Marlon dropped to the ring floor and turtled up expecting 'Gypsy' Jones to dive on top of him, but this wasn't a Mixed Martial Arts bout, it was bare-knuckle. Jones, the undisputed middleweight king of the bare-knuckle boxing scene, swaggered back to his corner and the smart-shirted referee started the count.

'1 . . . 2 . . . 3 . . .'

The crowd of five hundred or so roared in approval. 'Go on, Jonesy, my son.' As if some American homeboy could ever take their champ's belt away. 'Stay down, ya' washed-up twat.'

It was as if someone jammed a pitchfork into his side. As a veteran of more than fifty fights, 'Motown' Marlon Greene had been there before, but each shallow breath was like another stab to the ribs. So much for never showing 'em your hurt.

The thought of Tracy-Ann and the kids back in Detroit did nothing to ease the pain. It was just another Saturday evening for them, ordering pizza and watching a dumb movie together. Marlon didn't have anyone in his corner that night. The promotion wouldn't spring for an extra flight, and he needed the cornerman's extra money.

'4 . . . 5 . . . 6 . . .'

As Marlon struggled to his knees, he could barely hear the referee over the rabble. Out there, it was a sea of fading tattoos, bald heads and strange accents. They weren't the kind of guys that would shake your hand after the fight. He could smell their cheap cologne from inside the raised ring. Marlon would be going straight to the airport, or to the hospital — preferably the former. The pain was now an eight. Marlon blew out a sharp breath to reanimate himself. If he got on his bike for the next few minutes, he could get his wits back and would give himself a chance.

He had made comebacks in fights before. His greatest was a last minute 'triangle choke' submission of Scott Pickerman in front of a sold out arena in Vegas. That was back in the big leagues. Once a UFC title challenger, he was now reduced to taking any half-decent pay day: this one in some English town he'd never heard of. Still, a title would mean another fight, with money to

147

help keep his Detroit gym open. His friends and family asked him to hang 'em up, but you didn't turn down the chance to earn ten thousand dollars in one night. Now all he had to do was win.

'7 . . . 8 . . . 9 . . .'

Marlon looked at Jones parading along the ropes, already motioning for the belt to be put around his waist. He was a real animal — a shaved head, piggy eyes and cinder block forearms. He looked ugly, he talked ugly, and he fought ugly. During the previous rounds, the referee had ignored the illegal elbows and shots to the back of head, but Marlon knew that fights on the road were unlikely to be fair contests.

*Not today,* thought 'Motown' as he hauled himself back to his feet. He thumped his chest with his right hand and stuck his mouthpiece out at 'Gypsy.'

The noise level of the crowd dropped. They shuffled forward in their seats.

Jones couldn't hide his disappointment that he had more work to do that evening.

The referee peered at Marlon, who stepped toward him. 'Can you continue?'

'Yes, Sir,' he barked. Marlon looked down and saw the punch had landed right on the scar left by a twenty-year-old stab wound. The pain was fading.

The referee grabbed Marlon's wrapped hands and shook them. 'Ready?'

'Yes, Sir. I'm good.'

To have any chance, Marlon knew he would have to protect his body better, stick and move, and hope to land a good combination. Bare-knuckle sure was different to cage fighting — different distances, pace and footwork. Rather than staying in the pocket, fighters leapt in and out of range, throwing fastball shots at each other. After that prolonged attack, Jones would be tired, but he was still dangerous. Marlon knew at 37, his chin wasn't what it used to be, but he always arrived in good shape. Kickboxing, MMA, bare-knuckle: the rules didn't matter. He was a fighter, and he had another chance to get back into the 'W' column.

'Fight.' The referee clapped his hands together and Jones walked forward to the middle of the ring, head dipped.

Marlon bounced around the outside of the ring, getting his legs back under him. While Jones rushed in with wild haymakers, Marlon kept his cool and danced left and right, altering his movement. After a few range-finding attempts, Marlon landed some stinging jabs on Jones. According to the pre-fight prediction, the fight should have long been over. Jones was blowing, and came forward at a slower rate. Perhaps he had punched himself out. He definitely hadn't taken Marlon seriously — running his mouth, missing weight, and showboating to his fans — and now he was breathing heavy, stuck in forward drive like a broken tank. Marlon ducked a desperate overhand right and parried the wrecking ball of a left hook that followed. He was feeling fresher, and kept up his output of staccato bursts of punches. With one minute until the end of the round, Jones was slowing.

Now he was recovered, Marlon allowed his mind to wander. Sure, there were easier ways to earn a living — ones that didn't involve you shaving years off your life and dreading the next set of medical bills — but fighting was simple: your enemy stood right in front of you, and you did your best. Besides, fight week always delivered something Marlon craved, attention. Being recognized, being interviewed, and being part of 'the business' made it all worthwhile.

Jones plodded forward and Marlon played the matador, bundling him into the ropes. The crowd, robbed of their expected finish, jeered in frustration. Jones, now stuck in the corner, covered up and tried to put his legs back into gear. Marlon took his time, keeping his man trapped, backing off then jumping in with uneven combinations to upset his defence — right hook, right upper, left to the body, right straight. After fifteen seconds, the referee approached, looking for a reason to intervene.

The shouts of the spectators faded, and Marlon felt a lightness: a sort of elation. It was the same emotion he sensed in the seconds before the end of every one of his fights. *This* was where he lived — in the ring, or the cage, or anywhere where the crowd was on the outside looking in. *This* was where he was free to express himself. The last few years had seen his record slide from contender to journeyman, but he was still 'Motown' Marlon Greene, and this would be one of the good days.

'Keep your punches up, fighter.'

'Motown' continued pecking away with accurate shots like a vulture picking meat off a carcass. He stepped back and shot in with a thunderous straight right to the sternum. A shock wave of pain shot through Marlon's hand into his forearm.

Jones clutched at the ropes and fell to the canvas in stages. He rolled on the floor in agony.

'No knockdown. No knockdown.' The referee waved his arms in a low crossing motion. 'Low blow.'

*Was he kidding?* That punch was to the chest. The guy was holding his damned ribs. Marlon hung his head. It didn't matter what he said. This official was going to do his darndest to keep the belt around Gypsy Jones' waist.

The referee grabbed Marlon by the wrist and marched him around the ring. 'One point deduction. One point.'

A group of thugs in the front row made throat slitting gestures and threw their plastic cups. 'Cheating spook.'

He didn't expect a fair fight, but now he had a reason to get this over with. He couldn't wait to get on the plane home, back to the gym, the kids, even the debt. Normality.

The referee gave Jones the full five minutes to recover from the 'illegal' blow, and he came out for the last few seconds of the round refreshed.

Gypsy Jones removed his mouthpiece. 'Get the fuck off my turf.'

Marlon awoke to a bright light shining into his right eye. He lay flat, looking up at two paramedics and the fight official. *Fuck.* His right hand was broken and his jaw felt like it had been hit with a tire iron. He tried to sit up, but the official holding the flashlight pushed him back down by the chest.

'Unlucky, fella,' said the official over the noise. 'Fight's over. He got you.'

A weary Marlon raised his head a little and looked around the sports hall. He caught the same smell of cologne and stale beer, and saw the fans moving around in a buzz of activity. Some of them were still chanting. *God damn it.* Marlon wanted to be sick. Now he faced the hospital forms, prescriptions and another long layoff. Why did he let himself believe? Just for a few seconds, he had thought about that championship belt around his waist; imagined the calls from the sponsors; signed autographs for the first time in a long time.

The paramedics carried the stretcher out of the ring toward the double door. You had to take your losses and move on, but this loss felt final. Marlon closed his eyes and eased his hands behind his head. He wasn't ashamed of his performance, but he was tired of the nauseating losses and 'I told you so's'. Why did he continue to put himself through the pain and ridicule? That phone call to Tracy-Ann wasn't going to be fun.

# Dinner with Morris

*First published in Tall Travels*

We stood in the doorway, watching in silence, as Morris pounded the ball of pastry with closed fists. Little puffs of flour rose up after each strike. When he was satisfied it was flat, he picked it up and held it up to the light, causing it to sag. Then he started over again. When he finally saw us, he dropped the pastry on the kitchen top and it bounced onto the floor. His teeth arranged themselves into a grin. 'My dear neighbours. Do come in.'

Morris was a tall, wiry man of around sixty, with blue eyes that burned through his messy outcrop of white hair.

'Good evening, Morris,' I said, offering the bottle of Argentinian red I'd brought.

'Oh, thank you,' he said, taking the bottle. 'Lost the rolling pin, you see?' He then proceeded to sprinkle flour onto it and started using the bottle to roll the pastry. 'You must be the traveller, I suppose,' he said without looking up from his work. 'Returning to the parental nest, what?'

It wasn't the first time I'd met Morris, although he clearly didn't remember me. I was just an appetiser that evening — his neighbours' son. The guest of honour would be coming later.

My parents and I looked for somewhere to put our coats before they too were covered in flour. The place looked more like a hardware store than a kitchen, with drills on chairs and a couple of open cement bags next to the table — the remains of overcooked DIY projects. Half made picture frames and a host of other equipment lay abandoned on the floor. My parents looked at each other, but the polite social conventions of rural Sussex living prevented them from saying anything.

'Oopsy, I'll just make a bit of room,' said Morris as he hastened over to the table, clearing electrical cables and power tools as he went. It was going to be a long wait for the food.

The name of the place, Somerley Hall, may conjure up images of National Trust stately homes and Gainsborough paintings, but in reality, Morris's house was an old stone cottage, with a confusing mix of angled roofs and uneven floors. It also boasted a dried out fish pond and 'portholes' that he had cut into the hedges with a chainsaw. With the prospective buyer of the house joining us, most people would have tidied up, but most people were not Morris.

We watched, mesmerised, as Morris tossed unidentified cuts of meat and unpeeled vegetables into the pie. As he did so, he described yet more improvement plans for the home he was leaving, although they mostly seemed to consist of taking things apart and then forgetting how to put them together again. My father offered the occasional 'hmm,' to show that he was listening, but didn't entirely approve.

The doorbell sounded and our host scurried off to let the buyer in. 'Ah, there you are, David. Lovely to see you again.' Perhaps he was on his best behaviour after all, I thought. Morris showed the new arrival to the kitchen and dashed off to look for another seat as we introduced ourselves.

The buyer, David Hereward, was a portly, red-faced man, who was full of energy. My parents tossed up a few questions and he batted back the answers — from London. A Geologist. Holiday home for the family. They seemed satisfied with his solid defence.

Morris returned to the kitchen with a large white porcelain sink. He turned to David. 'I'm afraid you'll have to sit on this, old boy. The other chair's not so strong and you've got a bit of a tum.' The guest registered a look of surprise and stammered something about 'making the best of it.' At least he wasn't asking him to sit on the spare toilet that was on the back lawn.

The food still seemed hours away, so I suggested Morris open the bottle. He came over brandishing a corkscrew. 'The trick is to oxygenate it,' he stated, 'You can really unlock the tannins in the grapes.' Morris pulled the cork out and fetched a glass *carafe*. He showed his audience the bottle, then set the container on the floor and began pouring the contents in. He raised the bottle little by little, until it was above his head. The wine splashed against the rim and went all over his shoes and the floor. My mother rushed over to save him by bringing the *carafe* closer to the bottle.

He'd even managed to get it on his white top too. It was one of those rough cotton shirts that all sailing enthusiasts have. The difference was, Morris didn't actually own a boat. All he needed to complete the look was a red neckerchief.

Once we were safely sipping on our half glasses of wine, we tried to get to know David a little better. Morris interjected from the other side of the kitchen, like a misfiring cannon, 'A doctorate eh? My doctor told me I need to put on more weight so I should eat more butter. Trouble is I don't care for the stuff, so I've started putting double cream into my bacon sandwiches. Not bad eh?' And this was just one example. That man could meld any two words he heard into an unrequested anecdote or story. Fearing a new topic of conversation might be hijacked, we waited in silence, and sipped our aerated wine.

Morris decided to bridge the gap in conversation with some music, but rather than something relaxing, he chose a military march. We sat to attention and listened.

'Rousing stuff this,' he said. 'I find it perfect for work around house.' The blast of trumpets didn't seem the ideal backdrop for a dinner party to me. I noticed David looking through the window, out over the fields, dreaming of escaping to the Napoleonic wars, or some other historical battle.

The time for dinner neared and Morris laid the table as only he could. In front of every guest was a completely different set of crockery. David received a silver serving platter to eat from, my father had a children's fork with a steak knife and I got a thick terracotta plate, which looked as though it may have come in from the garden. As if double cream sandwiches and the high-diving wine were not strange enough, he served a bizarre array of side dishes to accompany the pie.

'What did you cook the mushrooms in, Morris?' my mother asked, with a well-practised smile.

'I simply added a spot of blackberry jam,' he replied. 'Had loads of the stuff leftover from last year and I thought I'd try something a bit different.'

'Well that's certainly a novel idea,' she said, subtly pushing them to the side of her plate.

The man was a real life Willy Wonka. He created oddities. He put things together according to his whims and wishes with no regard for tried and tested methods. At one point he drank the pie gravy straight from his plate and I started to feel like it was all a hoax, like it was a hidden camera show. I wanted to pinch myself to wake myself up, but I didn't need to. The acidic taste of the courgettes brought me back to earth. They had been flambéed in *Limoncello* — another one of Morris's improvisations.

With the marching band still blaring away on the stereo, David and my father took solace in the normality of discussions about house renovations and DIY. They considered the problems with the flood defences in the local rife, the correct way to wire underfloor heating, and the peak traffic periods for holiday makers.

'I've got a marvellous business idea!' said Morris, out of nowhere. 'Put more charging points in airports. People always need them these days, and the punters would pay a quid or two.'

'Well, a lot of airports do have them,' I replied. 'You don't normally have to pay f—'

'Yes, yes. More power is what they need,' he continued, rubbing the stubble on his chin. 'I know a contractor who could handle the work, perhaps I'll give him a call. I'm always having these little ideas.'

We moved on to a pudding which consisted of mystery stewed fruit with the host's favourite, double cream. We later discovered it to be persimmon, which he'd obtained for free from a neighbouring field. After desert, Morris insisted on showing us pictures of the boat he was hankering after from a local magazine.

'She's not seaworthy at the moment, but I'll have her ready in no time.'

'It looks like it may need some structural repairs, Morris,' said my father, who, as a navy man knows a few things about boats. 'I'd be happy to take a look at it for you.'

'No need old chap, I had a chat with the fellow at the chandlery, and I'm sure I can do the work myself.' Considering the chaotic state of his kitchen and his blatant disregard for power tool safety, I wouldn't have wanted to board the S.S. Morris on its maiden voyage.

We all declined the offer of coffee fearing that he might add juniper berries or caviar in another one of his inspirational culinary moments. We managed to escape just before midnight and David drove back to the sanctuary of his home in London, probably quite fast.

Strangely, the sale of the house went through without a hitch, and David has already started undoing much of Morris's handiwork, restoring Somerley Hall to its former glory. The last I heard of Morris, he had bought the boat, and was living aboard it in the marina while he made repairs. I'm not sure if his airport power socket business ever took off.

Thinking back to that evening, the strangest thing was how normal everything seemed to my parents. As we walked home they discussed the harvesting of the field and the Radio 4 schedule as if we hadn't just been to the Mad Hatter's house for tea.

# The Waitress

*Shortlisted for Writing Magazine's Music competition*
*First published in Scarlet Leaf Review*

When the lights dimmed, and Jake leaned toward the microphone, I knew in my heart he was speaking to me, no matter how many other people was there. Those eyes were the same deep brown as his beaten-up acoustic and his voice touched every part of the room like sweet cigar smoke. He played so gentle, like he was afraid he'd scare the notes away if he played too hard.

He'd performed about everywhere there was to play in Nashville. It was just a matter of time before someone picked up his record and gave it the attention it deserved. He never payed no notice of the critics anyhow; just kept on going.

Jake seemed far away even though the bar was small. Each new song he started added a little distance between him and the place, as if he was trying to escape. I imagined traveling alongside him on our road trip, his guitar in the trunk.

The press say he's too old to hang with the alt-country crowds. He's got a few miles on the clock is all. Fact is he's only thirteen years older than me.

His buddy was on accordion that night. Rich is one of the only people that didn't turn on him after that nasty business with his band, The Smithsonians. Hank was waiting at the side of the stage as usual. People are normally wary of Pitbulls, but he's a real sweety.

'Excuse me, Miss,' I said, 'would y'all mind keepin' it down? Jake's gonna play *The Waitress*.' Folks could be darned rude. Why would you come to a honky tonk if you just wanna talk all night?

That song was about me. I work in The Streetcar, a diner out on the 65. My momma don't make nothing, so we gotta pay the bills somehow. I'd had to beg for that night off so I could see the show. Melvin, the manager, said it had thrown the schedules out for at least a month.

Jake didn't give a damn about most of the audience, just saying the occasional 'Thank'ya.' The band spent years on the festival scene but they never got the exposure they deserved. They said Jake wasn't enough of a frontman. I didn't like the new singer, even if everybody else did. Jake closed his eyes and sang.

After the show, he was sitting behind his merch stand. We hadn't seen each other for two months, but I knew he'd been busy. He always answers my messages when he can.

'Great show tonight,' I said. 'Came all the way to see you.'

After he finished writing his note, he looked up. 'I thank you for your support, Shelby. I know I can always count on you.' He scratched his greying stubble, nervous like. 'Say, you wanna buy a pin?'

'Neat,' I say, looking at the badges with *Sell, Sell, Sell* printed on them. 'I can't though. Ain't got the money this month.'

'Mmhmm,' he said, 'I'm always a few hundred bucks away from living back in the truck. Singing don't pay.'

He was right. You had to be a social media expert to get a meeting with a label. Turning up together at the *Country Music Awards* was a while away yet.

'You gettin' any traction on the demo?' I held my breath, hoping for good news and a smile.

'No one willing to take a shot . . . but I got a residency starting at Nacho's grill.' He shrugged. 'Free tacos never hurt no one, right?'

I wasn't sure if he was kidding. Jake Sell should not be playing Elvis covers to restaurant diners. 'I know it is gonna happen for you this year Jake. Don't give up on us now.'

'Well, I don't know how to do nothing else,' he said fumbling in his pack for a cigarette.

A half an hour later, we went back to his apartment in his truck. The place was above a vintage store and the furniture looked like it came built into the place. Hank jumped into the armchair, leaving us two hard stools.

'Good luck gettin' him off there,' he said.

'You can't teach an old dog new tricks, right?' That one got a smile.

All he had in the cupboards was cookies, so he turned on the stove to make some tea. He lit a cigarette while we waited for the water to boil.

'What good country music boy don't have no family pictures?' I said. 'Where are your folks even from?'

Jake looked around for escape, but there was none. 'They ain't with us no more.'

I felt just terrible. 'I'm awful sorry, Jake . . . I wouldn't'a asked . . .'

'They was players too. Went on the road with 'em when I was young,' he pointed at some postcards on the walls.

We drank tea till late and listened to Leonard Cohen on his turntable. When we went to bed he said he didn't want to do it. It was the first time we hadn't been intimate. I didn't know what to think.

'I can't tonight, just can't.' He curled up in the bed like a cat backed into a corner.

'Guess I wore my best panties for nothin' then,' I replied. I knew he wasn't with anyone else. There was no second toothbrush in the bathroom. I even checked his phone while he took Hank outside to go pee.

\*\*\*

The next morning, he give me a ride to the diner. That day was real clear. I remember opening the window, feeling the cold air on my face. The crooked trees lining the highway were starting to straighten their backs for spring. The truck had one of those old-time radios with a manual dial. When you turned the knob to look for stations it crackled and fizzed. We got to the diner just on time for my shift.

'That'll be me then,' he said, starting the engine again.

I grabbed his hand and turned off the ignition. 'Come inside, darlin', you need a good meal, and I ain't takin no for an answer.'

He looked at his phone as if he had somewhere important to be.

'Get your butt in there, mister,' I said.

Thankfully, he obliged. Hank waited in the truck.

When he was seated in the booth and I had arranged my uniform, I came to take his order. 'Well hello there, stranger. Not seen you here before.'

'Quit it, Shelby. I ain't in the mood. I've only got about a half hour before I got to head back.' He usually liked my little jokes.

'Why y'all running back to town so quick? It's a Sunday.'

'Just let me get a look at the menu so I can choose.'

'Why do you want a menu when you got the best waitress in the state here with you. I'll bring you our special.'

He sighed and pretended to look defeated.

'You want some coffee while you wait?'

'You got red tea?'

I put on my smiling waitress voice, 'Sure thing, sir. Redbush tea comin' up.'

During the wait I saw him check his messages a bunch of times. Maybe he was nervous about having someone who cared about him so much. Jake wasn't used to folks wanting to share in his life. He looked even more distracted than the night before, sliding the salt shaker from one hand to another. When I brought the biscuits and gravy, he gave me a single nod of the head (that's Jake's official seal of approval). The dish was mighty big, but I never did see anyone who didn't finish every last scrap.

He didn't spend much time eating, and called me back soon enough.

'I gotta go, Shelby. Meeting in town.'

'Ooh, sounds mysterious,' I said.

'Well it ain't. Just some people that are important to me. Can't be late.'

'Well, all right. This meal's on me, and no arguments.'

He thought about protesting, but only for a second. 'That's real kind of you.'

'You're welcome to come by anytime. I mean that,' I said, trying not to sound like a mother asking her children to visit more often. 'Maybe I'll come into town next week, I always liked Mexican food.'

Melvin was peering through the serving hatch, looking for his star waitress. He didn't approve of all the yakin'.

'Shows start on the fifth. Six nights a week for the whole month.' Jake checked the clock on his phone again.

Why was he running away from such a sure thing? Was I not being obvious enough? 'Well, golly, I'll let you go if you really have to. You come by anytime.' If he ever came to his senses and asked me to move in, I could make sure he had more than cookies in the cupboards.

'Awful grateful, Shelby.' He scratched his head and pulled on his trucker cap. 'I'll be seeing you.' Jake could say so little and mean so much — those five words was like poetry.

He slunk off back to the truck and I got back to clearing tables. I noticed a whole biscuit left drowned under the thick gravy on his plate. He never did have much of an appetite.

\*\*\*

Those quesadillas at Nacho's grill was dry as hell. I don't know how they charged the prices they did. It was a fancy place I guess, with red and green decorations hanging from the ceiling.

After Jake's last show, we hadn't spoken. He just wouldn't open up to me, so I decided to give him time to think about what he was missing. I got busy working doubles at the diner and even went on a date with one of the cook's brothers. It was the longest Jake and I had ever been apart. He never did say much without a guitar in his hands, but I knew he must be missing me.

What he needed was an assistant — someone to make sure he got paid what he was owed, someone to hawk his albums, to contact promoters and labels. I would be able to give up waitressing and we could be together full time. I had it all planned out.

They had shoved Jake in the corner, like he was the side attraction to the 'build you own taco bar'. You could barely see him from the back of the room.

'I'd like to dedicate this song to someone special.'

I never did hear him dedicate a song before.

'It's called *The Waitress*, and today is a very special day for her. For us.'

A special day? It was March when we first met in Maddison's. He must have gotten the date wrong. It was a few days before our year's anniversary, but what the hell, at least he had noticed me come in. Maybe he was seeing sense after all.

He played the first chords, moving up the neck of his old Martin acoustic. He coaxed out the notes and sang that fine melody. That audience hushed up, and sat a little straighter in their chairs. The taco station was deserted. The song built up toward the soaring chorus.

*She was just a waitress in a small town,*
*But I'd wait a thousand days just to see her again.*
*I knew the moment she took my order*
*I wouldn't have no more reason to ever complain.*

Why had he never recorded the song? It was wonderful. The diners thought so too, and gave a generous round of applause.

'Thank you,' said Jake. 'Come see me at my stand if you like what you heard tonight. Enjoy your evenings, and Viva Nachos!'

There was a moment of still, complete silence in the room, before the yammering and the sound of forks on plates started up again.

Jake joined a table at the front, with an older looking woman in a smart dress, and a young boy. They was all smiling and laughing, although the boy seemed more interested in his chips than in what they was saying.

I waited a minute or two before I went over. 'Jake. Hey there, Jakey.' I waved as I approached.

He was all afluster, standing up, then sitting down, then standing up again to greet me.

'I *had* to come and check out your new show. The food ain't much, but the place is pretty nice.'

The boy looked up from his chips. 'I like the food. The food's nice.'

'Shelby is a big supporter of mine,' said Jake to the woman. 'Comes to all my shows.' She raised her eyebrows and he looked all bashful. 'She's a waitress too, you know?'

I wasn't worried by the competition — dark hair and hollow eyes with the onset of crow's feet. Without any food to pick at, she drummed her fingernails on the table.

She looked down on me, even though I was the one standing up. 'That's great, honey. Where do you work?'

'Err, a diner, out of town.' I laughed, trying to put a positive spin on it. 'Best biscuits in Nashville . . . well, that's what we claim.' She smiled all patronizing like. I wanted to say hello to Hank who was lying down between her and the boy, but he pretended like he didn't know me.

She reached for Jake's hand and smoothed it, 'You better learn how to cook, mister. It'll stop you getting into trouble with all these waitresses, writing corny songs.'

Corny? She wouldn't know a good country song if it smacked her right between the eyes.

'Shelby, this is my wife, Gloria, and my son, Chuck.'

How did I not know? He never talked about a wife or a son before.

'They just moved back to Tennessee after a few years.'

I didn't know what to say. He had ripped a tablecloth out from under me, and I was standing there, trying to decide which way to fall. 'Well golly, Jake,' I managed. 'Why didn't you say nothin' about your boy?'

'You know . . . we was apart for a long time.' So this was the part of him that was missing. I just thought he was private, that he didn't like me asking questions. But, in fact he had the answer all along, he just kept it secret.

'It's funny,' he continued, 'today is kind of like our wedding anniversary. We're gonna give it another shot huh, Gloria.' He flashed that smile, the real one I'd been waiting a year for, but it was for her, not me. My heart sank. I knew it wasn't no good hollering in a restaurant, but I wasn't going to give up easy.

'But I thought . . . I thought we could work together.'

He shuffled in his chair. 'Well, that sounds great, but I don't think I'm going to be needing no help. Turned down a tour opportunity with the New Forest Band and everyone's pretty sore about it. Got my hands full here you see.' He ruffled Chuck's blond hair.

'But that's what you've been waitin' for, Jake.'

He shrugged in defeat.

How could he just give up on his dream? Our dream. It sure would have been different if the boy wasn't there.

I went out for some air. Didn't want to give them the satisfaction of seeing me upset. Outside, I joined the smokers and coughed my way through a cigarette that some guy offered. I don't even smoke. It wasn't that late, and I didn't feel like listening to momma, with her chorus of 'I told you so', so I decided to head to Woody's to see if the acts was still going.

I knew in my heart that things wouldn't last with Gloria. You only get one chance, and she blew it years ago. Jake had his distractions, but he always came back to the music. Even if he didn't call for a week, or a month, or longer, I decided that I would be there waiting. There would be some time when he needed a good meal, or someone to listen to Leonard Cohen records with. He was my one, he just hadn't realized which waitress that song was really about.

# Wishful Thinking

*First published in Literary Yard*

Aiden McNealy tried his key in the door for the third time. Sodding thing always jammed. At least he didn't have to worry about waking anybody up. The teenage tossers downstairs had gone out, rather than DJing into the small hours, so his bedsit was quiet for once. After jiggling the key the right way, Aiden got the door open stumbled into the front room.

The beer festival had stopped serving at twelve and he'd even managed to get the last bus home. Last year he'd missed it, and had a three hour walk up the A429, with a few blunders into the Warwickshire hedgerows. That was a good one to tell the lads on the building site on Monday morning.

Although his workmates thought the Irish were all just pissheads, Aiden actually knew his stuff. He had been a member of the Campaign for Real Ale (CAMRA), since the 70s, back when nobody knew the difference between an IPA and an API. Whatever the year, he never missed the chance to try the latest award-winning brews. Beer wasn't just a 'cold one' to be cracked open at the end of the day, it was a craft, a work of art.

Aiden emptied the contents of his pockets onto the table next to the front door — a Nokia mobile, a few coins, and handful of losing tickets from the bookies'. He could smell the unwashed plates in the kitchen; he'd deal with them in the morning. He went through the plastic sliding door into the bedroom, kicked off his boots and flopped down onto the mattress on the floor, fully clothed. What was the point in paying £149.99 in Argos for a bed frame?

A couple more weeks in the flat would mark the third anniversary since the breakup. It had all come at once, Polly's affair, and Mary finding out she was adopted. The years had gone by, and it had been too damned difficult to tell her. He stared up at the ceiling. Polly might be gone, but he shouldn't give up on Mary. He'd have to dream up a pretty good excuse to go down south and knock on her door.

Things were looking up for tomorrow at least. After a full breakfast at the Big Eats Café, he would head onto campus for the four p.m. start. For those in the know, the university beer festival was one of the best in the area. It was mostly students wanting to get drunk and posing for selfies, but this year the Real Ale Society had sourced over a hundred beers from around the country.

He'd tried a good fifteen or so, and would try to sample the other new ones over the next two days. Before he could finish his prayers to the big man upstairs, Aiden drifted off into a dreamless heavy sleep.

\*\*\*

At quarter to four Aiden boarded the Stagecoach from Earlsfield to Warwick University.

'Day return please, fella.'

'£4.70,' the driver replied, without looking.

'I can't wait for me feckin' bus pass,' Aiden mumbled, dropping a fistful of change onto the plastic counter. He was running lower on funds than he had hoped. The 2:40 p.m. at Kempton Park hadn't gone as expected.

There was a free aisle seat on the top deck, next to a lady wearing a silk head scarf and beige raincoat combo. She offered him a smile as he sat down.

Aiden caught a glimpse of himself in the rain spattered window. Jesus. He looked rough as sandpaper. His face was a blotchy red, grey hairs bristled out of his nose and ears and his herringbone jacket looked tatty. He used to have muscles and a healthy glow.

The lady leaned in as if telling him a secret. 'Off to see my granddaughter at the university today.'

'Oh right.'

Mary had gone to university in Bristol and it seemed like yesterday that Aiden was a proud father at her graduation. The first McNealy to get a degree.

'It's lovely with her studying down the road,' the lady said. 'I never saw her much before, but now—'

'What does she study, like?'

'Sociology. Or is it Psychology? One of those I think.' She chuckled.

A man with spiky hair and a red shirt sitting opposite Aiden, leaned across the aisle.

'Blink and you miss it, eh? Then you're not needed any more.'

Very true. Aiden hadn't covered himself in glory as a father, but he had done a darned sight more than his da'.

'They're so lucky nowadays. I was out earning at sixteen.' Aiden thought back to the cold lunches and meagre pay packets during his carpenter's apprenticeship.

'I suppose you're too young for grandchildren,' the lady said.

'Well I've got one on the way, or so I hear.' He sighed. 'My Mary lives down in Devon with her husband, but we're not in contact much.'

'Oh that's a shame,' she said.

He gazed out of the window at the pattering rain. One mistake and his family had jumped ship, leaving him adrift, in Coventry. 'Families eh? What are you to do?'

The woman busied herself rearranging her bags, filled with supplies for the granddaughter no doubt. They sat next to each other in silence. Aiden checked his phone, but couldn't think of anything worthwhile to bother Mary with. He put it back into his pocket.

The festival was on the top floor of the blocky Student's Union building, in a bar called Zippy's. He shook off the rain, and climbed the four flights of stairs, wheezing.

He pushed through the double doors and was hit by the musty odour of beer and sawdust. Large beer kegs lined the walls with the cheap tables in front of them forming a bar. The Real Ale Society's crest hung above the small stage — *The 10th annual Warwick University Real Ale Festival.* The early drinkers looked at the new arrival, nudging each other as if to say 'watch out, Dad's home.' Most of the students were still probably in bed.

'Hello there. Are you a member of the Real Ale Society?' asked the smart alec on the door.

'Do I look like a student?'

'Well, you never know,' he said, sitting up straight. 'That'll be three pounds entry please. Do you know how the system works?'

'Yeah, yeah, use the cards to pay.'

'That's it,' he smiled. 'How many would you like?'

'I'll take four off you for starters.' Aiden handed over the twenty-three pounds and took the red cards from the student. 'Ta.'

Yesterday he had drunk a good few porters and stouts — the heavy stuff which reminded him of the old country. Today, he'd start with an IPA and try some of the golden ales. He fished out the guide from his pocket and wandered towards the far end of the long bar. Ringwood Circadian — that was it, the one he'd heard good things about. He hadn't made it this far down the pumps yesterday.

Removing the half-pint glass from his jacket pocket he held it up to the light. Clean enough, he thought. Half-pints weren't marked up like at some festivals. You could try a lot more beers if you drank halves. They ranged from one pound twenty to one-eighty. Not bad. 'A half of the IPA please,' he said pointing. 'You mind if I use me own glass? Don't like the plastic ones.'

'Sure thing, boss,' the lad replied. His gut was significantly bigger than Aiden's, even though he was only 20. His Real Ale Society rugby shirt had 'Big Mike' embroidered above the crest. He poured the beer into Aiden's glass, with just the right amount of head.

Aiden took a sniff — sweet summer. He brought the glass to his lips and swallowed half of it in one long gulp. A perfect mix of fruity hops with a slight bitterness underneath. 'Ah. Now that's real ale.'

'Oh yes, we're running out of that one already,' said Big Mike, crossing off one pound fifty from Aiden's red card.

Aiden heard a deep voice behind him mimic his Irish accent.

'Ahhhhhhh. Now dat's reeehl ale, boy.'

He did the 'half turn', managing to stop short of a full confrontation. From the corner of his eye, Aiden saw a tall, heavily-muscled type: blonde side parting, perfect skin, and a rugby team hooded top. The skinny girl clasped onto his arm was laughing.

Aiden was no coward, but on this occasion he decided it was best to ignore it.

'Some people are bloody fools,' he said to Mike, who was busy serving another customer. 'I just want to have a few decent beers in peace.'

\*\*\*

The bar had filled up, and the students had formed into their little gangs; groups from residential halls, sports teams, and a birthday party. The rugby lads, including the blonde one, were singing some awful songs.

Much to Aiden's surprise, the Real Ale Society had adopted him. It was always nice to have people to drink with, whatever the age difference.

'Where's your local then, Aiden?' said 'Scholesy', the ginger president of the Real Ale Society.

'The Star & Garter in Earlsfield I'd say. I'm there most weekends,' replied Aiden.

'Got anything good on tap?'

'Nah, the usual crap, Green King and Marston's I think. Cheap though.'

'You need to come along to one of our meets. We scout out the best pubs in Kenilworth, South Leam—

'We even went to Birmingham last month,' said a tiny Indian girl in the group. Her sweatshirt said 'Half Pint.' She was a token girl among the beer geeks, like your one off *The Big Bang Theory*.

'Where do I sign up?' said Aiden, mimicking a signature.

'No, really,' insisted Scholesy, handing a card to Aiden, 'we could do with a few members who really know their stuff.'

'Well, I've got the experience, like,' said Aiden. 'You lot are all right. You've got your heads screwed on.' He tapped the side of his head with a finger.

'It's my turn behind the bar in a minute,' said Half Pint.

'Oh you work it in shifts, do you?'

'Mmm hmm.' She nodded.

The posh idiot from earlier made an entrance. 'Anyone know where I can get some good head around here?' He guffawed at his own weak joke.

Aiden stared into his empty glass.

Scholesy turned and gave a forced smile. 'Nice one, Elliot.'

'You lot should come out with us, for rugby circle, if you can handle it. Lashings of beer on Wednesdays.'

'Well, it's more of a tasting thing for us,' said Scholesy.

'You lot should be called the Real Pussy Society.' Elliot looked back towards the rugby lads, who were hanging back, enjoying the show. He moved his attention towards Aiden, looking up and down, as if he had never seen an old person before. 'Isn't there an age limit on your society, Scholesy? This one looks like he could have a heart attack if he has too many more.'

'There ain't no limit, boy,' replied Aiden. 'I see they put a restriction on the Rugby team this year though. No IQ's above two digits.' Aiden bared his teeth at the Rugby captain, revealing a yellowed grin.

The hubbub of the bar did nothing to hide the silence that followed.

Elliot stood over Aiden, puffing out his chest. 'Am I going to have to watch you, Paddy? You might have a pipe bomb in that jacket.'

Aiden thought carefully about his next move. Maybe it was the liquid confidence that made him do it, but he was tired of being made to feel small (even if he was small). He leaned forward and exploded an imaginary bomb with his hand in front of Elliot's face. 'Boom,' he whispered.

Elliot didn't flinch. He looked down his nose with utter derision, then flicked his blonde hair out of his eye. 'I like you, Paddy. You've got balls.' He slapped Aiden on the back, a little too hard, knocking the glass out of his hand onto the floor. Elliot rejoined his teammates looking pleased with himself.

Aiden picked up his glass and inspected it. It was chipped. He turned to the group, who stared back, not knowing what to say.

Big Mike, who had done his turn behind the bar and finally had a beer in hand, changed the conversation. 'So does your daughter go to university, Aiden?'

'No, too old for that. Finished a few years ago.'

'Oh right. Managed to get a job? It's pretty difficult now.'

'She married a rich fella. We don't speak much on account of me putting me foot in it too much.'

'Oh,' said Mike.

Seemingly no amount of the 'hail Mary's' he uttered in prayer could save his relationship with his daughter. His last conversation with her must have been just after the wedding. She didn't want his 'guilt money', and told him not to bother calling again. He still hoped she would come around, and that one day his mobile would ring.

'I want to do a Master's after I finish anyway.' Big Mike shrugged.

Aiden tapped Mike on the shoulder. 'Don't be in no rush to join the real world. I haven't been out of work a single day since I became a chippy, and I got nothin' to show for it.' He checked his watch. It was nearly ten-thirty. 'Time for another,' he declared, leaving Mike pondering his future studies.

The barman had changed. Or had he? Aiden had sunk enough beers that he wasn't quite sure. He could be that bloke from the bus earlier — black hair, red shirt.

'What's this one?' said Aiden, pointing at an unbranded keg at the end of the bar. 'It wasn't here before was it?'

'You don't want that one,' the barman replied with his twinkling smile and perfectly gelled spikes. 'You'll regret it in the morning.'

The room was packed now and the noise made it difficult for Aiden to hear. 'What is it?'

'It's called Wishful Thinking. It's a concept beer. It has a pretty strong effect.' He hadn't let his smile drop one inch. The barman leaned over the bar and put his hand across his mouth in a kind of 'aside'. 'It's only for the open minded, not for sceptics.'

'For better or worse, I've always been a believer,' said Aiden looking heavenwards, 'and I never pass up the opportunity to try a new drop.' He held out a red card for the barman to deduct the right amount.

'Are you sure? You'll notice the effects tomorrow.'

Aiden pushed his card forward again. 'Bring it on.'

'If you're sure.' The barman waved away his card. 'This one is one me.' He checked around to make sure no one else was watching, then opened the tap and poured a pint of gloomy looking beer into a plastic cup.

'Grand. Thank you kindly.' Aiden grabbed the glass. He took a long pull on the pint, finishing around a third of it. It was a full bodied, fruity beer, it tasted better than it looked. 'Not half bad,' he said, looking around for the server. But, the barman had disappeared.

There was a little space at the end of the bar, and Aiden sipped his pint. It had been hours since he had eaten, but the microwave meal that waited for him at home wasn't exactly appetising. He'd

177

probably manage to burn it anyway. With his back to the bar, he tipped the last drops of golden brown liquid into his mouth.

Suddenly, Aiden's head was spinning. The air in the room turned thick, like molasses. Then with a flash of bright light, the barman appeared from nowhere, right in front him.

'What the—? How did you—?'

The barman brought his face right up to Aiden's. 'Finished I see, my good man. Now for your wish.'

Aiden blinked, taking a pace back and bumping into the bar stool behind him. 'What is this? A wish?'

'Straight up,' said the barman, raising his jet black eyebrows, 'make a wish. Anything is possible with a bit of Wishful Thinking.'

'I don't believe in that bollocks. Magic cards and hokum pokum. It does nobody no good.' He was ready to turn his back on the barman and head home.

The barman reached out and touched him on the shoulder. 'But you said you were a believer, friend. Tell me your heart's desire.'

Aiden straightened up. One little wish couldn't hurt. He thought back to his chipped glass, and that jumped up rugby player calling him IRA. Ignorant prick. He clenched a fist and crushed the cheap plastic cup in his hand.

There was another flash of pure white light in front of Aiden, which temporarily blinded him. He screwed up his eyes and steadied himself on the bar. The next thing he knew, that very rugby captain was moving in on his spot, lining up the bar for a picture.

'Budge up there, Paddy. I want to get a picture for the team Instagram.' He muscled into the tiny space next to Aiden, squashing him against a group trying to get served.

Someone shouted 'Selfie with the leprechaun.' They were taking the piss now. Just because he was older than them, didn't give them the right to take the bloody piss.

Elliot held his phone up at a jaunty angle and pouted. Adjusting the angle, he crouched down and planted a wet kiss on Aiden's stubbly cheek.

Aiden turned. 'What the feck do you think you're doing, laddy?' he shouted.

Elliot looked back at him in mock surprise and said in a badly mimicked high pitched voice, 'Where's your little pot of gold then?' He looked back to his group of mates. They were loving it.

Aiden hadn't come out to be slobbered on by a sixteen stone Country Life gobshite. Snorting like a prize bull, he squared up to the young man and took aim. It had been a long time since he'd punched anyone. Must have been way back in his twenties. Right foot back at a forty-five degree angle. He shuffled his left foot forward, and raised his hands.

Elliot was still grinning back at his mates, fiddling around with his phone.

Aiden leaned back, pushing the students at his back, probably spilling a pint or two. He transferred all of his weight forward, windmilling his right fist in a huge arc. His hand felt like a mallet searching for a peg to thwack into place. The punch seemed to take days to reach his foe, making its way from below his waist, around and over his shoulder, towards Elliot's smug face. This was going to be good. Aiden's fist found its target, just behind the ear, where the blonde side-parting was combed down. There was a satisfying crack, and a tingling sensation spread up Aiden's forearm.

Elliot's head snapped to the left and his body tensed. Just as Aiden thought he was going to spin around and return fire, he flopped to the sawdusty floor, like a barrel of bricks being emptied. He crumpled to his knees, then his shoulder whacked against the bar and spun him over. The captain of the rugby team lay on his back, staring blankly up at the ceiling, having just been decked by a sixty-year-old.

Time seemed to speed up. Aiden had to think fast. Nobody had reacted as yet. Most of the bar hadn't seen, and were still chatting away. He crouched down and slapped Elliot's sleeping face. 'Night night, Prince Charming.' Reaching into Elliot's hand, he removed the phone, which was still on camera mode. He lined up a shot of his pallid unconscious face, and pressed the capture button. 'Beautiful.'

A prompt appeared on the screen on the phone in Aiden's trembling hand.

*Post to Instagram?* He didn't give it a second thought. Aiden hit *Yes*, dropped the phone, and headed for the exit, before anyone started asking questions.

***

What was that throbbing pain? It felt like a car had run over his right forearm. Aiden tried to open his eyes, and with considerable effort, they pinged open one after the other. He lifted his hand in front of his face to inspect the damage. Bleedin' hell, it was twice the size it should be, and felt twice as heavy too. Great, he was going to have to spend his whole Sunday in the hospital waiting room.

What had happened after the punch? How had he got home, and why didn't he have a hangover? It didn't matter. He vaguely remembered the Ale Society lot helping him onto the bus and him promising to go to their next meeting in Coventry. Good lads.

Aiden scooted his legs off the mattress, straight onto the carpet. He still had trousers and white vest on. At least he had taken off his jacket and boots. He turned over and got to one knee, then two, then stood up grabbing onto a curtain to steady himself. 'Ahh, Jesus!' he screamed. He had used his right hand to grab it. *Idjit.*

The hand might have hurt, but it wasn't going to fall off. He may as well make breakfast first. He remembered to use his left hand to open the sliding door into the small open plan living room with galley kitchen. The kettle had enough water in it for a cuppa, so he flicked it on.

Making his breakfast omelette wasn't going to be easy with one hand. Putting his hand on the fridge door handle, he moved to his right so as to open it with his left. Then he saw it — the graduation photo fixed to the fridge door. It was something he looked past every day, but that morning, he really saw it. It showed the McNealys, back in the good old days; before Polly had left, and Mary had stopped thinking of him as 'Dad'. That was his moment of achievement, the high point before he had become the Irish stereotype, either at the bookies' or the pub.

What a fool he'd been to waste his wish on clocking that big ponce, rather than fixing things at home. He needed a lot more help in that department. That barman was right. He did regret the pint, free or not.

Aiden felt the cold coming from the fridge which was still open. He sighed. The breakfast could wait, so could the bleedin' hospital. Today was the day to fix things. What should he say? Where should he start? He wasn't sure. He would have to wing it, but the gift of the gab was the one thing that still hadn't deserted him.

He dug his phone out of the opposite pocket with his left hand, with some difficulty. He brought up the number and pressed the call button before he had the chance to back out.

The phone rang. He listened. A few rings more. Maybe she wasn't going to pick it up.

'Err . . . Dad?'

'Hello, Mary love, it's your Da' . . .

'I know, I have caller I.D. What is it that you nee—'

'Just listen. I've got some things I want to say.' Aiden settled down into the tattered armchair in the lounge and gazed skywards, looking for help. This wasn't going to be easy.

# Balcony on the Fifth Floor

*First published in The Fiction Pool*

*In a few minutes they'll be here.*

Martin stood frozen to the spot as his colleagues rushed around him. He cracked open the plastic lid of sparkling water, listening to the fizz of the bubbles. Why was the newsagent out of San Pellegrino again? He'd had to settle for a brand he'd never even heard of. It would probably be flat in no time. Two prescription strength ibuprofen tablets went down the hatch and his hand felt for the plastic seal around the new pack of Benson & Hedges in his pocket. He didn't know if he would get a chance to open them before the meeting.

Martin was about to deliver the biggest pitch of his career. Winning the business would mean he'd finally get *that* bonus — the kind with a lot of zeros. Without it he may as well cut his losses and walk away from the company, even after fourteen years. The cocky little twerp in charge of tenders at PWC would soon be there with his team of stern consultants. The client was a hot-shot with an MBA and a few years of experience at an international recruitment firm. He spoke in acronyms and percentages. He wanted results and wasn't interested in how they were obtained. Creative ideas would be a hard sell. Martin would have to play nice and flirt with him a bit. Everyone was gay in the glamorous world of advertising weren't they? Either way, it wouldn't hurt to boost his ego a bit.

The gangly intern returned from the copy room with ten neatly bound pitch documents: *Creative recruitment solutions for PricewaterhouseCoopers*. He handed them to Shelley, the frizzy-haired New Business Manager and withdrew to his corner desk. She flipped through one of the folders hoping to find an error she could highlight, but found no good reason to make a scene.

Martin pulled open the French door and walked out onto the fifth floor balcony. It was his favourite place in the building — so close to the buzz of the office, yet it felt a million miles away. Everyone knew not to bother him out there. He was able to shut the door on all of the bullshit and think, if only for a few minutes. He'd had some of his best ideas pacing up and down that two-by-five metre space, imagining the river Thames beyond the buildings which blocked his line of sight. It was only halfway to a good view.

You weren't supposed to smoke out there, but no one was going to tell a director off. He sparked the lighter and held the flame over the end for a little longer than he needed to. He closed his eyes and inhaled deeply. Nicotine wasn't going to kill the headache, or settle the feeling in his stomach. He'd spent weeks working on the briefs with his team and had even come into the office on Saturday to make sure the work sparkled.

Down below an endless line of black cabs crawled along Sloan Street. A bike messenger with a poster tube slung over his shoulder weaved in and out of traffic on his fixed wheel bike. Why did people ride around on those death traps? Once you got going there was no back-pedalling, no changing your mind in a hurry.

Why couldn't they be pitching to Lavazza or Rimmel London? Writing copy for Associated British Ports and Londis wasn't what he had dreamed of all those years ago as a student in Bournemouth. Were the clients even serious about switching their business? They were probably doing this for a better deal. The bastards.

Last night at the club Gavin had been whispering into a young cub's ear. He couldn't have been more than twenty-four. Gavin had probably fucked him. After nine years of late nights, drugs and promiscuity, the thought of growing old with him suddenly filled Martin with dread. What would happen when he got too old for his Sunday club residency at Hex? What are gay Londonites supposed to do when they pass forty? Move to the country and get a Labrador and a Land Rover Discovery? Balls to that. Martin imagined the gossip at the neighbourhood Christmas drinks gathering. A couple of queers living in one of Buckinghamshire's quaintest villages — that wouldn't do.

Martin felt his stomach tense. His head throbbed. The comedown from last night's pills was starting in earnest. He'd been a fool to pile onto the 07:20 train with all of the other commuters after only three hours of sleep. He caught a glimpse of himself in the reflective window. He was also losing the battle of the bulge. At six feet two he was well-built, but his midriff was considerably looser than it once had been. He had thrown on a crumpled shirt that still smelled of smoke. His tortoiseshell glasses were last year's trend, and grey hairs were slowly taking over his beard.

Martin forced down the bile rising in his stomach and took another cigarette from the packet. He felt dizzy. Staggering, he steadied himself on the balcony handrail and closed his eyes. His head was spinning — swirls of purple and green. The tinnitus acquired from years of DJing rose to a scream in his right ear. There was a reason the Brixton community called them suicide Mondays.

'Are you OK Martin? . . . Martin?' Somebody was knocking on the French door. 'The clients have arrived.' It didn't matter now. Martin kept his eyes closed. Although he didn't want to step back into reality, he would have to go through the office and past everyone to make it out of there. Martin braced himself for his escape.

He turned and tore open the sliding door, pushing past a young Art Director, hurrying towards the lift. He hammered the elevator button repeatedly but the light remained steadfast. Floor number two. Stairs it was. Martin leapt down them two at a time. It seemed like fifteen flights even though it was only five. He finally made it past the reception desk out into the Knightsbridge air. The shoppers and pedestrians continued about their business, disinterested in the tall paisley-shirted man having a panic attack on the pavement. They gave him a wide berth and went about their business, while Martin rested his hands on his knees and fought to regain his breath.

After a minute the Creative Director opened his eyes and straightened up. Martin began to stride away from the office building. He ignored the phone buzzing in his trouser pocket. He kept walking. He had no idea where he was going.

# The Seventh Day

*First published in Flash Fiction Magazine*

Lawrence Ashby shuffled over to the kitchen table in his charcoal-coloured dressing gown. He had difficulty bending his right leg these days. He put his mug of camomile tea down next to the *Bath Chronicle*. The sounds of choral music drifted over from the radio.

'We buried a pair of babies at the crematorium today,' he said to his wife, Agnes. 'Twins. It was very sad.' He took a small sip of tea.

'Little twins? Oh dear,' she replied, standing at the kitchen sink.

'And a lady who had made it to 'the big one hundred'.'

'Oh yes?'

'I suppose there's not too much to hang on for after that.'

Agnes put the casserole dish back into the washing up bowl. 'Well, it's just a number after all.' She swept the silver hair from her eyes with a rubber-gloved hand, and got back to scrubbing the plates.

'I'd like to go to the cinema tomorrow.' Lawrence stood and

moved to the window, gazing out. 'There's that new *samurai* film.' The dark curtain of evening had begun to obscure the bright flowers in the garden. 'We could go for a meal afterwards. What do you say?'

'Hmm, I've got those library books to return, and then there's the shopping.' Agnes gave him a resigned smile.

'Perhaps I'll venture out on my own, make the most of my day off.' He straightened the two cacti on the window shelf and swept some excess soil into his hand, then dropped it into the bin, covering the tea bags. He returned to his seat and turned past the obituaries to the cinema listings in the newspaper.

'Let's have a look. Four-thirty, six or nine.'

The telephone rang with its long, persistent tone.

'Can you answer it, Love? I've got my hands full here,' said Agnes.

He reached over to the sideboard and picked it up. 'Lawrence Ashby speaking.' Over the next minute, he gave a series of short, clipped answers into the receiver. 'Yes . . . I see . . . all right . . . all right. I'll be there at eight.'

'Who was it?' asked Agnes.

'Humphrey's got laryngitis again. It looks like I'll have to cover tomorrow.'

'Oh dear. It's a shame about your film.'

Lawrence replaced the receiver carefully. 'I was looking forward to a day out of the suit. This'll be seven in a row.'

\*\*\*

'I'm sorry for your loss,' said Lawrence, extending his hand with its gold sovereign ring on the little finger. 'Lawrence Ashby. How are you?'

The family took it in turns to return the undertaker's warm

greeting.

'Would you like to wait inside? Or perhaps you'd prefer to look around the gardens.'

They mumbled a response and wandered off to look at the flowers.

Lawrence limped up to the building with his ebony cane. The previous group of mourners had finished in the chapel, and he busied himself ushering them towards their cars, with the final words of thanks and sympathetic smiles. Although he was a patient man, there was a schedule to adhere to. Six funerals a day was no easy task, but he always got proceedings started on time.

Long past retirement age, Lawrence sported a significant paunch and a grey beard that was thin enough to have been called 'whiskers' in Dickensian times. He had the perfect posture for the job — bowed forward in a show of compassion — and he brought character to Timsbury Crematorium, as only a wizened local could.

When the family returned from the gardens, he approached them, pulling up gracefully like a hearse. 'I have the Orders of Service ready.' He opened up the box and began to hand one to each family member.

One of the grandchildren suggested passing them around in a chain to make it quicker. 'Oh, that's fantastic,' Lawrence said with a grin, 'I hadn't thought of that. Wonderful.' Of course he had thought of it. He passed each one out as if they were certificates.

When he was finished, Lawrence took a step back, finding the perfect distance to maintain. He felt a light breeze through his socks where his wide-legged trousers didn't quite meet his polished shoes.

Taking his top hat from its familiar resting place on the stone pillar, Lawrence showed the bereaved to their places in the chapel. There was only a handful of them. It was a sad fact that most of the deceased knew very few people by the time they passed away. He positioned the hat on top of his wispy hair before entering.

When everyone was seated, and Father Stephen had started proceedings, he directed the pallbearers to deliver the coffin. They put it down on the plinth, bowed and departed, never facing away, leaving space for him to pay his respects.

Lawrence removed his hat with both hands. Standing centred in front of the coffin, he bowed from the waist, arms straight down, the hat gripped by his side. He held the position, perfectly still. After five seconds, he would normally have straightened up, and given a curt nod, before heading out of the chapel exit, thus completing the ritual. But this time he couldn't straighten up. He felt a vice-like grip high in his chest. He couldn't breathe. What was happening? It was as if a strong magnetic was pinning him to the floor. Lawrence dropped to his knees. He tried to say something, anything. No sound emerged, his lips just flapped like in the silent movies.

The mourners looked on in astonishment. Several seconds passed. No one could believe that their service had been hijacked. Rushing to help him would put an end to Grandma's funeral.

For Lawrence, this certainly wasn't the day off he had planned. The undertaker turned his head and looked up from the red carpet, past the pews and through the heavy wooden doors. Instead of thinking about his childhood, his prized flower garden, or his wife Agnes, he wondered if that *samurai* film was really as good as people said it was.

# Raft

*Winner of the Writing on the Wall
Festival Flash Fiction Contest 2018*

A large African man looks around the office. It's stripped bare apart from the table and chairs. Even seated, he is almost a head taller than the man with a uniform and a name badge — Juan. The two men look across the table, through the silent steam of the teapot.

Juan inspects his fingernails and weighs up his first move.

'Do you need a translator?'

'No. I speak your language.'

Juan removes a damaged photo from a plastic wallet. 'Can you tell me about this?'

The man remains silent, his features muted. He reaches for the photograph, then changes his mind.

'We need to identify them. Do they have documents?' asks Juan.

'No documents. I cannot help you.'

'We can speed up your application,' says Juan.

The man bows his head and begins to cry. Juan busies himself pouring the teas.

'That's me in the middle,' the man says between sobs. 'The whole village is there.' He swallows. 'Now only me.'

It's been just one day since the crossing from Libya. The hours huddling together felt like years, clinging on while the raft was tossed about like a cheap paper plate.

'And who was with you?'

'Son, daughter, and my brother's family. My wife stay at home.' A tear rolls down the man's pudgy cheek and narrowly misses the paper photograph. 'You cannot tell her. You must not—'

'Can you write the names for me?'

The man writes the names.

Juan reaches across the table and rests his hand on the man's for a second, then removes the paper.

After a pause, Juan speaks, 'We want to reduce the deaths.'

The man looks up, through watery eyes. He shakes his head.

'Who did you pay?'

'I cannot.'

'Think of what you came for. A better life,' says Juan, smiling.

The man is not listening. 'I tried to drown, but my body don't let me.'

'Who put you on the boat?'

'They kill me.' He draws a finger across his throat.

'Anything you can tell us. The payment, the dates, any face you remember . . .'

The man shakes his head again.

Juan sighs and takes out a packet of cigarettes. 'We need to keep the photo, for identification. I'm sorry.' He slides the photo back over towards the plastic wallet.

'No.' The man catches his hand and stops him.

'You'll regret it if you don't tell me now,' says Juan. 'There is no more time.'

'What does time matter to me? You people will still be asking the same questions in a hundred years.'

The tea sits between the two men, untouched.

# The Change

*First published in 'The Ripening',*
*National Flash Fiction Day anthology*

Patrick had loved burgers ever since he was old enough to cram them into his mouth. He loved hotdogs, wings, ribs and steak too. Then one year, during his physical, the doctors told him he better stop eating meat, or he'd be next to go.

His family and friends wondered if the Burger Shack would survive without him. It did, and without visiting his favourite heart-attack drive throughs, Patrick lost eighty pounds. He took up jogging, visited the national park and bought a whole new wardrobe.

Patrick ate things he'd never considered before — multicolored beans and unpronounceable berries from Asia. He brimmed with energy. Why wasn't everyone vegetarian? He wanted to shout it from the hilltops, but he punched in at work every day with his shirt ironed and his lunchbox in hand, counting down the days until he could escape to the national park. Greeting other hikers was exhilarating; like there was the secret club he'd been missing out on his whole life. It wasn't long before Patrick was taking half-days from work to feed his desire to visit the wilderness.

One Sunday, Patrick drove to the park entrance, waving to the rangers as he arrived. He changed into his running kit and set off on the long loop. It was a crisp day, and he had the trail to himself. His legs pushed him up the rocky path. His new thighs were solid rock whereas the old ones would scream for oxygen just climbing the stairs. Patrick continued up the steep trail, anticipating the endless view of blues and greens from the top.

On the final ascent, Patrick's legs began to slow. Each step took greater effort, and when he looked down, he saw that his skin was turning gray. His legs were now weathered stone and it took an enormous effort to pull them the final few steps. As he reached the top his heart beat like thunder. What was going on? A rooting sensation traveled through his abdomen, into his chest. He lifted his shirt to reveal his midriff; it was woody and gnarled. This solid oak chest no longer rose and fell with each breath. The earth was claiming him. A strange euphoria coursed through Patrick's arms and into his fingertips, tightening his muscles as it did. Moss and other greenery sprouted from his hands. Only his head and neck remained free.

Unable to move, and with no-one within earshot, Patrick was helpless. Yet, rather than scream and wave his head around, he stood and watched. He took a final breath of pure mountain air and observed how the hills, the rocky outcrops, the woods and meadows all melded together. Patrick stood with the landscape. His vision clouded over and then his head was still. He was home.

# Overlooking the Lake

*Highly commended in the Reflex Fiction Spring 2018 competition*

The first time he sat on me, John Lovelace was a young man. He was a straight-laced, straight-A graduate with a new job in the zoning department. John used to eat his lunch in City Hall Park, overlooking the lake, alongside other workers sitting on *their* benches. He never changed places. He didn't like change. His brown paper bag contained the same every day — a peanut butter sandwich, a granola bar and a red apple. He would drink from the water fountain when he was finished.

One sunny day, Marta joined him on his bench, and while he brooded over his sandwich, she feasted on a colorful salad. Marta asked if he was going to finish the other half of his granola bar. John laughed and handed it over. The next day, she brought an extra piece of cake in case John wanted a change. He did.

They developed a routine, exchanging pieces of their lunch and married the next spring. Every day at one o'clock, they sat and shared fresh baguettes, homemade chutneys and olives that came from expensive-looking jars. Gone were the peanut butter sandwiches. When their first child was born, Marta stopped coming to the park, but John continued.

After a few years, I noticed John's backside expanding. He went from tubby to plain overweight pretty fast. Fewer people joined him as there was less space on the bench.

One Monday, John didn't bring his lunch to his spot overlooking the lake. He wasn't retirement age and I knew he wasn't on vacation either. A month later, Marta returned to where she'd first met her husband. She had a brown paper bag with John's name on. She carved their initials onto my armrest with a pocket knife, then she sat and cried. Marta removed a peanut butter sandwich from the bag and hurled it into the lake. She never came back after that.

Unfortunately, J.L. and M.L won't be together forever. The City Council are replacing all us benches with vandal-proof plastic ones. There was nobody left at the zoning office to deny the application.

# Frozen Stiff

*First published in Flash Fiction Magazine*

'Look, that dog is asking for money!' Timothy pointed at the thick-furred husky with a plastic pot clasped between his teeth.

'Don't give money to dog. Is lazy man ask for money.' Anya clicked her fingers and hurried on with her clipboard raised, robbing the dog of its best chance of a meal that day.

The children filed along the snowy pavement with their heads bowed. One of the boys stamped his feet with every step to combat the cold seeping in through his soles. The two girls in front followed the tour leader obediently, silently, with their hands jammed deep into their pockets. Anya turned and gave them a warming smile.

It was only nine o'clock, but this was the second time Timothy had held up the group. Earlier it had been to interrogate a businessman who was buying his breakfast: a litre of strong beer. They would never beat the crowds at this rate. The group turned right onto the arched bridge that would lead them over the river towards the Hermitage museum.

'Do you know, children, if you look at every exhibit for ten seconds, how long would take your visit?'

Before the children could guess, Anya halted, noticing the black and yellow tape across the raised middle section of the bridge. She instinctively unfastened the belt from around her black woollen coat, widening her profile and trying to block the children's view, but it was too late. Timothy stood on tiptoes, straining to see what was in the road. 'What's the man doing?' he enquired.

The body on the pavement was sitting bolt upright with his arms clamped to his sides, as if bound to an invisible chair. His face was a fiery blue, his body frozen rigid under wet clothes. He looked like a toppled shopfront mannequin. It was unlikely that he'd willingly taken a bath in the Neva and then hauled himself up onto the bridge. He had been left there for all to see, another trophy killing.

Anya hoped, prayed she wouldn't recognise the face. She steadied herself on the railing and drew breath, sucking in the cold air. She shepherded the group back towards the main road, flapping at them like a swan with wings outstretched. 'We must take other way, children. This way not open, is closed.' She monitored their little faces and watched as the colour drained slowly from them. The girls in front nodded, with watery eyes.

She quickened her pace and motioned for the children to do the same. It would add at least ten minutes to their journey, and she needed the sanctuary of the museum with its audio guide headphones and gift shop trinkets to take their minds off what they had witnessed. At the back of the group Timothy raised his hand hopefully.

'Yes, what is?'

'Can we go back and see to the dog again? I found some money for him.'

# The King's Last Meal

*First published in Laurel Magazine*

People think it's all about the hair, but it's more than that. The rolled up sleeves and mirror sheen shoes take plenty of preparation too.

The cell door opens.

'You look fabulous, Pressley,' he jeers, as he puts the tray down. 'Here's what you wanted.' Johnson is the worst of 'em, a freekin' tyrant.

'What about some music?' I ask. 'Ain't heard nothin but *Rock Around The Clock* in the library, and that's just a cliché, man.' I shovel in some mashed potato and gravy. It's not the same as the Roadhouse Diner, but it's alright.

'Just eat your damned meal and be grateful.'

'I'm innocent, man. Why should I be damned grateful?'

He pretends not to hear.

Being a greaser used to be a thrill. Friday nights at the Roadhouse, breaking rules and badmouthing our shitty bosses. But,

201

dressing different ain't much advantage here; it's just a drag, everyone raggin' on me, calling me Elvis and shit. I never even liked the guy.

'Hey Johnson, got any tattoos?' I show him the skull in front of flaming checkered flags. He raises his eyebrows all sarcastic like. 'Got that one way back, ' I say, 'before my girl really screwed me put me in this dump.'

'From what I hear, you weren't the only one she was screwing.'

Nobody talks about my Wendy like that. I throw the tray and drive my shoulder into his gut. He's quick with his baton and I'm licking my wounds in the corner before long.

He finally recovers his breath, grinning. 'Clear your tray, Inmate. You won't have to put up with this dump much longer. Nearly time to meet your Rock 'n' Roll heroes.'

I sigh and clear up. Another fine dining experience is over, my final one. It's been a hell of a few years in this place. Don't know which is worse, the physical beatings or the courthouse ones. I think back to the Christmas variety performance. Maybe I should've just played along with what the others wanted — Jailhouse Rock — might have even made a friend or two. Guess it's too late now. I may be going down as guilty, but truth is like the sun: you can shut it out for a time, but it ain't going away.

# FOREIGN VOICES

# Thanks

I would like to thank everyone who has helped me on my writing journey. These people include my friends, family and my writing associates in Alpha Writers. A special thank you goes to Sarah Clayton who helped with proofreading. Finally, thank you to all of the people who took the time to read this book.

# About the author

Philip Charter is a writer and teacher who lives and works in Spain. He is tall, enjoys travel, and runs the imaginatively named website 'Tall Travels'. His fiction has been published in literary magazines and anthologies, and his piece 'Raft' won the 2018 WOW Festival flash fiction competition. He is currently working on his second collection of short stories.


Website: philipcharter.com
Twitter: @Dogbomb3
Facebook: philipcharterauthor

Printed in Great Britain
by Amazon